EYES
FULL OF
EMPTY

JÉRÉMIE GUEZ

Translated from the French
by Edward Gauvin

The Unnamed Press
Los Angeles, CA

The Unnamed Press
1551 Colorado Blvd., Suite #201
Los Angeles, CA 90041
www.unnamedpress.com

Published in North America by The Unnamed Press.

1 3 5 7 9 10 8 6 4 2

Copyright 2013 © Jérémie Guez
Translation Copyright 2015 © Edward Gauvin

Originally published in French as *Du Vide Plein les Yeux*
by La Tengo Editions in 2013.

ISBN: 978-1-939419-43-9
Library of Congress Control Number: 2015950955

This book is distributed by Publishers Group West
Printed in the United States of America by McNaughton & Gunn

Designed & Typeset by Scott Arany
Cover Design by Jaya Nicely

This book was translated and published
in part thanks to support from The French
Mission for Culture and Higher Education.

EYES
FULL OF
EMPTY

"So what do we do now?"

"Shut up. I'm trying to think."

—James Belleck,
Red Clay Visions

PROLOGUE

So today's my birthday.

On a stool, elbows on my knees, head in my hands, I wait for the feeling to go away. This joint has fried my brain. Hash so bad you have to squeeze the glowing end till your thumb blisters, just to break it up. All so it can do you the service of shoving a rod through the middle of your skull, scattering thoughts good and bad and indifferent, mowing down everything in sight. This fucking piece-of-shit hash has done time in plastic wrap, pockets, socks, probably even someone's ass, before getting fobbed off in the yard. A gift horse from my cellmate, Tarik. I told him it was my birthday today, and he handed me the joint and said, *Have a happy one, on me.* I really lucked out with him. When all you have is a hundred square feet to live in, better get along with the guy you share it with.

"Gonna take a shit," says Tarik.

I turn the lighter on an orange peel I keep in a plastic box under my bed for times like these, to freshen up the cell as needed. I watch the peel blacken, flames running down the coarse grain. I take a deep breath, filling my lungs with smoke. It smells like citrus and ash. I am seriously high.

Odds were almost zilch a guy like me would end up in prison. On paper, I was spotless. My dad thought he'd steered me down the straight and narrow; to be fair, he'd nearly killed himself to make it happen. He'd come looking for me whenever I was hanging out on the stoop or somewhere else in town, messing around with the guys from the neighborhood. When I turned eighteen, it seemed like he'd won. I went to college. The old man, happy at last. His integration now 100 percent successful. A guy who'd grown up in a podunk village in the Djurdjura mountains—limestone everywhere you looked, a lunar landscape where he wore out his shoes each morning walking miles to the only school for natives. A kid from Buttfuck, Algeria, born to illiterates, who'd ended up a French citizen. And a doctor.

You're Kabyle. Don't you ever forget it. He'd said that over and over to me, all through my childhood, clinging to his story even while occasionally denying it. I never forgot, which didn't keep me from fucking everything up. All those stories I never wanted to hear again—all I wanted was to hear about my mom, who wasn't Kabyle or French, just Absent, with a capital *A*. You catch on quick when your dad doesn't know his way around members of the opposite sex. It starts when you grow up without a mom. You might see a few random women over at the house, but they never get asked to stay for dinner. And then you never see them again.

The toilet flushes. Tarik pulls back the curtain and heads over to his cot. He lights a cigarette and watches TV with the sound off, as is his habit.

I don't blame my father for anything. I don't know anyone who had a better dad than me. He knows it too. That's probably why he took my time so hard. Six months, no appeal. I can still see the expression on his face in the courtroom. He looked more shattered than me when the judge pronounced the verdict. Assault and battery: *Guilty.* Premeditated aggression: *Guilty.* Didn't think the asshole would press charges, or that I'd hit him and he'd start choking on his own blood. Or that his dad was the head of a huge media conglomerate. I didn't see any of it coming. But in the end, half a year isn't so much out of a whole lifetime.

I borrowed a book from the library. The author was an ex-con. All told, he did more than a dozen years inside. It's like some people are made for prison. Is that possible? He says he never thinks about it at all anymore. He also says he's known people who just did a few weeks for some bullshit—a license infraction, a scuffle with a brother-in-law—and they never get over it. I'm one of those people. I'll never forget this as long as I live, I already know it. I don't blame society. I don't blame the justice system. I blame myself, just myself, for having been so goddamned stupid. I wanted to be a tough guy. Every day I wake up and remember I'm just a little turd here, a fact soon confirmed in the exercise yard, where I'm at the very bottom of the food chain.

Eyes glued to my shoes, I hear a shout from the hallway. I pay no attention, don't even realize the shouting's louder than usual, until Tarik gets all excited.

"Oh, holy shit! Look at that!"

I look up at the corner of the cell with our commissary-bought TV. I see the images, but my brain isn't processing them. A plane *in* a skyscraper. A commercial jet. A massive building. Tarik yells, "It's New York!"

We have no idea what's going down as we turn up the volume and start listening to the news. Word spreads swiftly from cell to cell, dumb rats in cages given a bit of a distraction. The guards tell us to shut up. They shouldn't have raised their voices. And suddenly, it's on. All the prisoners start going at it: blacks and whites, reds and yellows, believers and everyone else with no god but their dad and a few belt-whippings for their sins.

I celebrate my twenty-fourth birthday behind bars, my only gifts the worst joint I've ever had and the first major disaster of the new century, joining everybody else in the world with no fucking clue of what's going on. So I start screaming too, as loud as I can, half hoping the tears will come, but they don't. And it wouldn't change a thing. I just want to do something. Because I wish the planes had crashed here. For once, something's going down; I'm not about to miss out. Happy birthday my ass. They can all go fuck themselves.

TEN
YEARS
LATER...

CHAPTER 1

IF THERE ARE SOME PEOPLE YOU DON'T SEE ANYMORE, IT'S usually by choice.

When he called, I didn't recognize the voice and he refused to give his name. He said he had some work for me, paid well. I said meet me at the café across from the Rex, the movie theater. I got there early, to be sure I saw him coming. The sun glared down, too hot for September. Call me a typical Parisian. We complain when it's not nice out, and the minute it is, we start saying it's too hot, our city isn't made for this.

When I see him, I instantly regret accepting the meeting. My only hope is he's not the asshole who called and he'll just walk by. No such luck. He sits himself down across from me and checks out my hairline. I started losing my hair in prison; these days I comb what's left over my forehead and hope against hope. Soon it won't make a difference. I'll end up like my dad in a year or two, bald at thirty-five. One last slap in the face, to prove once and for all I'm actually part of the family.

He grins like he knows all that. "Idir! You haven't changed a bit!"

I shift in my chair, preparing to bolt. He looks just like he used to: same face—the face of an entitled teenager who refuses to grow up—scraggly mustache, blue eyes, and dirty blond hair brushed back. How many times had I seen him strut that long, skinny frame of his around on TV, talking about the news like an appliance salesman gushing over the latest bagless vacuum? Oscar Crumley. I've known him for ten years, give or take. His mother's French, a former model. British father, a Francophile, came over after a brilliant career and found himself head of a media conglomerate. Naturally, Oscar is a consummate asshole. The kind of guy who—not dumb, exactly—can give indignant political rants while blasted on champagne, nostrils rimmed with powder, at a party in some palatial apartment overlooking the Jardin du Luxembourg. Back in the day, he lived like a Saudi prince—every night fucking girls I could barely dream of asking for a light. If there are guys you want to headbutt each time they open their mouths, then Oscar's one of them, no doubt about it.

These days his dad's wearing adult diapers in a five-star clinic, waiting to quietly die, while Oscar's graduated from TV personality to corporate boss. The guy I used to be jealous of is now "the biggest media mogul in France." Son of a bitch, I ate prison food for six months because of him.

"Got a nose job, I see." I can't help but point this out. He hadn't really had a choice. I'd pretty much beaten his face in.

He grins back, no apparent grudges. "Well, you broke it in three places."

"I was a rookie then. My hands were overenthusiastic." Back in the day, going to college for me was like parachuting into hostile country, a descent at once swift and secret. Unlike the other kids in my class, I needed cash. Sure, my dad fed me and kept a roof over my head. But I wanted money, money to burn. Because a bottle in a club on the Champs-Élysées was no malt liquor from your corner bodega. Because fucking cost money, cost champagne, cost meals, cost weekends in Italy. I was a lazy ass, still am. So I started doing people favors they were too embarrassed to handle. The favors became more complicated, more sensitive. Without trying, I'd become your basic fixer. And then a friend came along asking me to cave Crumley's face in. Why not? At the time, I thought I'd done a thorough job. My friend was satisfied. Then Crumley had the nerve to track me down and identify me, which got me arrested for the first and only time. His decision to press charges put me in prison for half a year. Pathetic as sentences go, but enough to fuck a depressive like me over good.

The waiter shows up. Oscar orders a coffee, asks if I want anything.

"No thanks."

Less than thrilled, the waiter pulls an about-face.

"Let's get this over with. Who gave you my number?"

"Morel. He spoke highly of your improved skill set."

I scowl and look around for more pleasant things to stare at than Oscar Crumley. Ten years ago, I didn't have much of a choice when I got out. My father told me to come home until I could get back on my feet, get a job, rebuild my life. But I couldn't do that. Not after prison. So I made the most of my network and my early reputation, which my jail time had only solidified since I never snitched on my client. The rich have a habit of solving their problems in a very civilized way. Of course, in a pinch, they might call on some actual hoodlums. Their business. But usually the rich are afraid of guys like that blackmailing them once the job's done, having too big a mouth or too heavy a hand. If Morel had paid some bangers from the projects to take care of the little shit harassing his daughter at school, they might've beaten the kid to death, which would've led to a whole ton of bullshit. Me, with a jerk like that, I pay him a visit in the foyer of his parents' Haussmann town house, slap him around a bit, make him sweat. Problem solved.

I give the rich an easy answer to their problems. I speak their language, understand their needs, and guarantee things won't go too far. I also have boundaries: I've turned down several murder contracts. My job is very simple. I follow women, sometimes mistresses, for jealous men. I watch over kids for worried parents. If it comes to it, I threaten people sometimes, but that's it. I'm not a gangster and I never will be. It's all a matter of scale. On the streets, I'm a huge pussy, but for these people, I'm the big bad fucking wolf. I own my little niche market and, so far, I've had no competitors; no one's come up with the shitty idea of trying to horn in on my territory for a measly few thousand euros a year.

"What do you want?" I finally ask.

"As I said before, I have a job for you."

"You really think I'd take it?"

"Look, we were young." He uncrosses his arms in a conciliatory gesture. "My father pressured me to press charges—"

I wave away his excuses. *Please stop. Stop before I burst into tears.* I want to tell him to piss off, go fuck himself. I want to absolutely destroy him again, just for kicks, because I feel like it and I still can. But I hold back. I don't have the balls, and I need money, as usual.

"Two hundred euros a day, plus expenses." I aim high, pick a number at random.

"Sure," he responds right away.

Dumbass me—money just got left on the table. I tap my foot impatiently. "OK, I'm listening."

He reaches for his messenger bag and pulls out an accordion folder, the kind with the rubber band that snaps around. "I'd like you to find my brother—my half brother, I mean. His name is Thibaut. I haven't heard from him for two months. No one knows where he is. It's all in here."

He slides the folder over.

"Your dad's son?"

"Yes. When my mom died, he remarried." For a second his face tightens, like he's trying to swallow a horse pill without water. You'd think he wasn't really into that part of his past. Like he's watching his stepmother, just a few years older than he is, playfully ruffle his dad's hair over breakfast right now.

"Does he know? That your brother disappeared I mean."

"My father is quite ill. The slightest shock could send him over the edge. My stepmother is the one who came to see me. I told her I'd take care of everything."

"Tell the police?"

"He's an adult, twenty-two. They say he'll turn up on his own."

Times have changed indeed, I think. Back in the day, the Crumley family could make anyone rethink their opinion. Even a judge. "School?"

"Same as us."

"So he'll go into business, like his big brother?"

Crumley smiles. "I'm a broadcaster."

"Can I see his mother?"

"No, I'd rather you didn't. It wouldn't do any good—it would just complicate things."

I nod, used to stipulations like this. "The customer is always right."

For a second, his left eyelid gives a nervous twitch. He pulls his wallet from his jacket, opens it, and removes four five-hundred-euro bills, fanning them out on the table. "Call me in ten days."

"Got any bigger bills while you're at it? Shit, man, I don't live in Auteuil, you know. How am I supposed to buy anything with these in my neighborhood? They're gonna think it's funny money."

He pulls a face, implying I'm as big an ass as I ever was, and leaves me alone at the table.

———————————

It's hard to argue with the money in my wallet. It lets me pick up some produce and eat something besides Tuna Helper. My sublet's on a little street leading to place Pigalle not far from the café where I met up with Oscar, so I decide to walk home, a plastic bag of groceries in each hand. I get a stitch in my side going uphill toward Saint-Georges, which sucks: I don't smoke and hardly drink, but big-ass me is out of shape all the same. My building has no elevator, and I live on the sixth floor, so by the time I'm back home I slam my door shut and collapse on my fake leather sofa. I look through the file Oscar gave me. The first thing I find in the accordion folder is a photo—a portrait of Thibaut Crumley. Most likely an enlargement of something taken at a party. He's got a three-day beard and tortoiseshell glasses, and is staring in all seriousness right at the camera, like he's posing for a fashion mag. He looks like half the young guys in town.

I empty out the rest of the folder's contents on the coffee table. His transcripts. I give them a quick once-over. Conclusion: he was a good student. A pair of keys with an address in the Marais—probably his apartment. Oscar could've told me his brother didn't live at home anymore. I would've headed straight over.

I rouse myself, ready to leave, when my cell phone rings. "Hello? Good, and you? What, tonight? Oh right, *iftar*. No, of course I haven't forgotten."

I'm lying. I've totally forgotten. Tonight is the last night of Ramadan, and my grandmother has summoned me to dinner. "Don't worry," I promise. "I'll be on time."

I take the metro to République and walk to rue de Bretagne, where café owners wear aprons like the wholesalers at Rungis, except that around here rent must be pushing a thousand euros a square foot. I don't have the keypad code for the building, so me and my brown face hang around out front until a little old lady opens the door. I go in behind her, giving her the nicest smile in my repertoire so she won't think I'm going to rape her and her tiny dog in the closet where they keep the trash cans.

I check out the mailboxes. No name tags. Why don't students ever put their names on their mailboxes? Do they not know that court summonses never come by e-mail? Fucking maladjusted children.

Five floors, two doors on each landing. I start up top; students always live in the garret. I run into the little old lady again, unlocking her door. I make like I don't see her and try my key on the door across the way. No dice. Fourth floor, key works on the first try. I turn it slowly in the lock and push the door open with my foot. The apartment's huge. But I knew that. One look at the lobby and you knew; you don't need a real estate broker to tell you. The kitchen opens on the living room, American style. A long hallway, a door on the right: his room. Nothing special. A closet with some clothes inside. Books lining shelves built in above a desk. A full bed, flawlessly made. I peek underneath. Among the dust bunnies is another accordion folder. I have to get down on the floor to reach it. Inside are a dozen cassette tapes, unlabeled. It's strange. The only loser of his generation who didn't switch to MP3s? Impossible. A sound distracts me from the tapes and I shove them back under the bed. I hear the same sound again, same volume. Moaning. I poke my head out the door to see where it's coming from, treading lightly now. There. A second door at the end of the hall. I take a deep breath and bust through—not much point in knocking.

Only the girl sees me. She quits her back-and-forth and turns her head my way, neither scared nor embarrassed, still perched on the guy. She's pretty, with a phenomenal ass. His eyes are still closed, and he starts pumping away twice as hard to make up for her stopping. Walking in on people having sex is never pleasant, but over the years I've mostly gotten used to it. When you go poking into other people's shit, you are, unfortunately, confronted with this kind of scene more often than you'd like. I enjoy watching her ass shudder for a split second longer before he notices I'm there.

"The fuck you doing here?"

Jolted from romantic rapture, the guy shoves the girl off his dick, gets out of bed, and makes a beeline for me, looking all threatening, unimpressive boner preceding him. As if to compensate, his muscles are huge, horrendously sculpted by a serious weightlifting regimen and, undoubtedly, the abuse of questionably legal substances.

"Get out of my apartment or I'm calling the police!"

I laugh. "Your apartment?"

In my younger days, I used to know a bodybuilder. One night we wound up drunk in a dive near Porte de la Chapelle. Some bikers were partying there. Given how big my buddy was—he must've had the prettiest triceps in the whole Goutte d'Or—I thought we were in no danger. I don't really remember what started the fight—probably a bad joke the bikers didn't get. We got our asses kicked. Well, my buddy did. He couldn't run fast enough to get away. I could. All this is to say it's hard for me to take seriously guys all swollen up on protein shakes who can't throw a goddamned punch to save their lives.

I slap him once, hard, with my palm. He whimpers.

"What'd you do that for? Are you crazy or something?"

I move forward. He sticks his hands out to protect himself.

"I'm looking for Thibaut. The fuck are you doing at his place?"

"I—I'm his roommate."

And here I thought he lived alone. I'm learning something new every minute. "What's your name?"

"Charles."

"OK, Charles, I just want to ask you a few questions. I'll take two minutes of your time, and after that, I'm out of your hair."

"OK."

"How long has it been since you've seen Thibaut?"

"I don't know...two months? Maybe three."

"You're not worried?"

"No, he's kind of...special. Sometimes he vanishes for a week or two at a time every now and then. Keeps to himself. His dad pays his share of the rent, so...can I put my clothes on?"

"He have a girlfriend?"

The kid doesn't answer, just stares at his feet. The girl, who I'd forgotten was there, answers for him. "Yes."

"You know her?"

She gets up from the bed and walks toward me, her full breasts pointing proudly my way. "That's me."

"Get dressed, we're going for a coffee. I'll wait for you down-stairs." I turn my back on her. "Thanks for the help, Charles. And a piece of advice—lay off the steroids, they shrink your dick."

I wait for the girl in the lobby. She takes her sweet time com-ing down. Naturally, when she does, she's all made up. "What's your name?"

"Eve."

Just Eve.

"OK, Eve, you know the neighborhood. I'll let you pick the café. Seeing as it's going to cost us an arm and a leg, it might as well be a good one."

We sit down on a terrace. I get a good look at her up close. She's prettier than I thought. Brunette, olive skin, big green eyes. "What're you having?"

"A café crème."

I pass it on to the waiter, who drifts off.

"Aren't you having anything?"

"I'm not thirsty."

She nods vaguely, clueless about the holiday, but why should she? For someone like her, fasting's what you do when you've just bought a dress a size too small and have a big party the next night.

I let her think another minute. I don't want to rush her; I have the feeling I'll need her.

"So you're not a cop?"

"No, Thibaut's brother hired me to find him. You know him?"

"I've run into him before. Does that mean you're some kind of detective?"

"No. It means I'm looking for Thibaut. You got something to tell me about him?"

She shakes her head. "Nothing special. He was kind of secretive, like Charles said."

"You try and call him, ask him where he was?"

"Yeah. But he didn't pick up."

"And you don't care?"

"Sure I do. But I'm not worried."

What with the scene I walked in on earlier, it was hardly a surprise she was in no hurry to see him again. "What kind of relationship did you have with him?"

She gives me a look like I'm the biggest dipshit on the planet. "Um, we were dating?"

A lull in the conversation. She doesn't seem to understand what I'm after. Or her mind is elsewhere.

Eve's eyes flare defiantly: "Call me a slut if it will make you feel better."

"What, because you're sleeping with your boyfriend's roommate after he's been gone for two months? No, not at all." I laugh despite myself. She gives me a dark look. I won't be getting anything more out of her. I signal the waiter for the check and drop a five-euro bill on the table.

"Thanks," she says.

"Keep me updated. Call me if he turns up." After exchanging phone numbers with her, I let the girl go and start walking, trying to put together what I've gathered so far. No one appears to be worried about Thibaut's absence, and I don't know much about him. He seems to be a stranger to his brother, and not much more than that to his friends from school, never mind his girlfriend.

By the time I reach home, I'm convinced the kid will wind up coming back on his own; he'll turn up as soon as he needs some cash. When you've lived in a huge apartment in the Marais, it's hard to turn your back on comfort and slum it bohemian style.

I lie down on my sofa, fully intending to keep thinking about the case, but I fall asleep. When I open my eyes again, it's dark out, and I'm late for my grandmother's.

With my free hand—the other one busy with a box of pastries I bought at Barbès—I knock on the door. My grandmother opens up and a smile lights her face from ear to ear. Her Berber tattoos stretch on skin that time and a life spent looking after her own have creased with wrinkles. Lines on her temples, her chin; crosses on cheekbones—all traced in ink, now faded. Indelible markings to protect her family from the evil eye and mourn her deceased husband. These are tattoos that visibly irritate my father, though they seem to have worked. I've always liked them.

"You came! *Mashallah!*" she says.

She kisses me on either cheek. A long hug, then she loosens her embrace. "Come in, come in!"

"Here—for you." I hold out the pastries; she takes them from me without a word of thanks.

"Hurry up! Give me your coat. They're all here and waiting on you to eat."

"Who's they?"

She doesn't reply. From her silence, I realize it's not just my father, which already doesn't exactly thrill me, but other family members too. And since I can only stand so much of them, I have to give the old woman credit for not telling me they'd be here.

She lets me walk into the living room alone.

"Good evening." There's my father; his brother, Aziz; Aziz's wife, Anne; and their son, Dmitri, who's in his early twenties.

I start regretting not asking my grandmother more questions about tonight. Still, what was I expecting? After all, you can't take the "family" out of "family dinner."

I go around kissing cheeks, finishing up with my father, who slips in a "How are you?"

"Fine. You come alone? Where's Nadia?"

"She, uh, had a lot of work she couldn't get out of."

Nadia's been with my father for going on ten years now. But he still balks at inviting her over, like his people, his tattooed mother and thug son, aren't good enough for a brilliant French-Moroccan lawyer.

"Hiding her, eh?" I say in a moderately unpleasant tone.

I can't stand the people in this room, and since my father's worth more than all the others put together, I take it out on him first. He says nothing. I sit down at the table, which is laden with all sorts of dishes. Anne smiles at me and asks, "Makes your mouth water, doesn't it?"

Anne's one of those people hooked on all things Oriental. As soon as she became a teenager, she knew she'd marry a foreign guy, if only to piss off her parents. And yet she named her son Dmitri. Even people like that can't take too much of the exotic. I've never been able to stomach her comments—they seem plucked right out of travel guides she's spent a little too much time poring over.

Instead of answering, I just shrug, not yet resolved to engage in hostilities. Of course it's mouthwatering, especially for people like me who work during the fast. I pour myself a glass of lemonade and toss it back in one gulp, telling myself that at this point, dinner can still go well. But she keeps laying it on: "Aren't you hungry?"

"No, no. I haven't eaten all day, but I'm fine."

My father gives me a dark look.

"Kidding, just kidding."

"We haven't seen you in a while. Ramadan go well?" my uncle asks.

"Yes, it's done me a lot of good. I needed it," I reply, meaning it. My grandmother brings the last of the dishes to the table and serves us all soup. The sucking noises start. I should never have come. I try to put it all behind me and focus on my bowl, sneaking glances at the others now and then from the corner of my eye. The conversation has a hard time getting started. I can feel my presence making everyone uneasy. I decide not to overplay my role as an asshole, even if today has seriously gotten on my nerves, and for the good of everyone present I toss off a "How's work, Dad?"

"Fine," he says, a man of few words.

My uncle bravely tries to run with it. "How about you, Idir? What are you doing these days?"

"Oh, helping people out here and there. Odd jobs. You know, the usual. Nothing out of the ordinary."

"Did you know your cousin signed with a record label?"

I don't like people who ask a question just so you'll have to ask them the same question back, even though you couldn't give a fuck about the answer. "No, really?"

Dmitri gives me a shy little smile.

"*Mabrouk!* How'd that happen?"

Anne tells me her son's success story, tears springing to her eyes.

Unlike my father, who accepts who he is, my uncle's always been ashamed of his origins and just loves playing the perfect little Frenchman. He raised his son to be the same way. From the way Dmitri's hair falls over his eyes and the grossed-out look he gives his soup, it looks like my uncle succeeded.

"Careful, I hear music can be a dirty business...drugs and all."

"Your son never lets up," my uncle tells my father in Kabyle.

I take it up with him in French. "Hey, you think he can't speak up for himself if he doesn't like my comments? How about it, Dmitri? You'd tell me, right?"

Dmitri blushes, mutters a quick, *"Oui."*

"There, you see? And speak French, will you? Or else your wife and son won't understand a word you're saying."

"You're such a little shit," my uncle says.

"Uncle, if you've got something to work off, we could go settle this outside."

"That's enough," my father says, rising from the table. "Get out, Idir."

I get up before he has to repeat himself and duck into the kitchen to kiss my grandmother good-bye.

She reaches up and her dry hand settles on my cheek. "Idir. Take care, slow down."

"Gotta run, I'll stop by tomorrow afternoon."

Before she can respond, I dash out of the apartment, slamming the door behind me, relieved.

———

On boulevard de Clichy the next day, I stop by a call shop. I don't have Internet at home. When I need it—and it's just for work—this is where I go. Seated at his desk, the owner, a young Pakistani of about twenty, is playing with his cell phone.

"How's it going, Anam?"

He looks up at me and smiles. I like it better when his wife is minding the shop. She should be starring in a Bollywood movie, not running a cybercafé that caters to losers and pervs.

"Idir! Good, and you?"

"I need a computer."

"Make yourself at home." He waves me into the room, where four computers are lined up against a wall. There's no one else around. I sit down at the last one, open a browser, and start searching. I type in the name Thibaut Crumley and get a Facebook page plus several newspaper articles. Photos of Oscar and Thibaut, arm in arm. And their father, the three of them together, a family: "We're very close..." It hurts to say these words; the brothers' smiles are forced. I check the dates; the oldest article is less than a year old. All very recent. Nothing particularly interesting, just PR bullshit. The problem with my line of work is no one ever tells you everything. Otherwise, the kind of people who pay me would never call on my services. It's something I've learned. A kind of tacit agreement. The client sits down across from you and tells you his problem with its share of lies and gray areas. There's no point asking for explanations; you won't get any. It's part of the deal.

I switch off the computer and push the chair back under the desk.

"How much do I owe you?"

"Done already?"

"Yeah."

He laughs and tilts his head. "I don't have a minute rate. Forget about it."

"Thanks, my man. Have a good one." I leave, touched by his gesture. I should stop chatting up his wife.

I decide to head up to Abbesses for my first coffee of the day, sort out my ideas. Seated on the café terrace, I pull out my cell phone.

"Hello?"

"Hey, Eve. It's Idir. The one looking into Thibaut's disappearance."

"Yeah, I remember."

"How's it going?"

"Fine. Is there something you want? I already told you everything I know." She doesn't sound delighted to be talking to me.

"You guys ever go to parties?"

"Uh..."

"What I mean is when's the next one you have lined up on your social calendar?"

"Saturday."

"Think I could stop by, speak to some people, y'know—"

"You want to interrogate people?"

"No, no, just drop by, talk a little. We could go together if you want."

She doesn't really seem into that. "I don't know if that's a good idea."

"What if I brought a little something along?"

"What do you mean?"

She knows exactly what I mean. But maybe I'm wrong about her, and she doesn't partake? I add, "The party favors will be on me. Free. All you have to do is bring me to the party and say I'm a friend. That's all. I won't hassle you."

"OK," she says quietly. I wasn't wrong.

"What time should I swing by?"

"I don't know, ten? Eleven?"

"Where do you live?"

"In the Sixth. I'll text you my address."

"Great. See you Saturday." I hang up. Now I have a window of opportunity to find out a bit more about the kids at the party.

It's not much, but at this stage, things could be worse. At least I'm making progress, which can feel rare in my business when you're trying to pay the rent. All I have to do now is score some drugs.

I set course for Belleville. Why go all the way over there to score when I live so close to the Goutte d'Or? Well, I have my habits, and it gives me a chance to visit an old friend.

I step into the bar at the foot of the boulevard, walk past the counter, and spot Hakim at a table with two other guys. He gets up to greet me. I give him a kiss on either cheek, then extend a hand toward his two associates.

"You here to see Tarik?"

"Yeah."

The only way to see Tarik is through the guys who work for him.

"Sit down, grab a coffee. I'll call him."

With these words, he pulls his phone from his pocket. I head back to the bar and order a coffee. I'd had some nasty preconceptions about Tarik when they moved me to the cell he'd had all to himself till then. I felt like a poacher on someone else's property. I was scared stiff and he could tell. I made a total mess of everything. He turned out to be a good shoulder to lean on. It was a relief, spending six months with a guy like him, on the quiet side, only spoke when he felt like I needed to hear someone's voice. He was used to prison; it was an integral part of his line of work. He was just past forty and he'd already spent a dozen years behind bars. A telephone allowed him to stay in touch with his men and watch over his territory, which small-timers were always trying to cut in on. So he spent most of the day "at work" and left me the fuck alone.

Hakim comes back and says, "He'll be here in a few."

"OK, great. Thanks."

I sit down at a table off to the side, pick up the sports pages, and flip through, sipping my gross coffee. Paris St.-Germain F.C. on the front page. A couple dozen million for a young Brazilian player. I like my team as much as ever, but I can't stand how hip it's gotten. I bet in a few years there won't be any more genuine PSG fans, with seat prices going through the roof. I bet they'll make us play at the national stadium, that piece of shit. Fuck, we came to see some soccer, not the four-hundred-meter hurdle.

"No way! It's the little Kabyle, back in his hood!"

I look up, and Tarik's standing in front of me all smiles, hair slicked back, face closely shaven. Seeing him always puts me right back inside, where I was constantly in fear of a crying fit coming on. The fact that it never came I secretly attribute to Tarik's friendship.

I get up, and he clasps me to his muscled torso for a long hug and asks, "Another cuppa joe?"

"No thanks."

"You know Ramadan's over, right?"

"I just had one. It'll do me. Got a delicate heart." I smile back at him.

He sits down next to me and shouts at the owner, "Admer, coffee, please."

"Looking good."

"You too, buddy. So what brings you over?"

"I need to buy a little something."

He looks at me, astonished.

"Not for me, asshole."

The waiter brings his coffee over. Tarik knocks it back in one gulp. "I don't get it."

I lean over closer and whisper, "I have to find this kid. His folks are loaded, you know how it is. His friends are throwing a party Saturday and I want to bring a present."

Tarik stifles a laugh.

"Come on man, this is *work*."

"Sorry, I just can't get over it. Damn, so even bougie kids go missing. But I don't see how I can help you."

"I want to get them talking, and I can't think of a better way."

"You want to be the man with the candy?" He busts out laughing again. I shut up and wait for it to blow over. He must be able to tell from my face I'm getting impatient.

"Sorry. It's just I haven't seen you for a month, and now you show up with this story."

"Can you help me or not?"

"Of course. What do you need?"

"Well, uh, I don't know. What do you think this crowd is going to want?"

"Wait a sec, Idir—where's the camera? You come see me and you don't know what you wa—"

Exasperated, I crank the volume up a notch. "It's not like I'm the dealer here!"

He shakes his head sadly. "Yell a little louder, why don't you? I don't think they heard you at the other end of the bar."

I start in again, more calmly. "How about some blow?"

"Are they bougie?"

I nod.

"So bring some X and a few pills. On top of the coke, I mean."

"That's fine. I trust you." I get up and put my jacket back on. I leave a two-euro coin on the table for the coffee. "Put something together for me?"

"Yeah, sure."

"When should I come round?"

"Don't worry, I'll have it dropped off."

"Thanks. I'll be by to pay you in two days." We trade cheek kisses.

"Don't worry. You can get me back sometime. I never forget, you know."

"Cut it out with that shit. You're the one who helped me out back in there. I never did a thing for you."

"You always came by for visiting hours after you got out, even when my own friends stopped showing up. I don't need any more than that."

———

Once I'm outside the café, I head back to the Tenth to drop in on my grandmother instead of going home. On the way, my phone rings. I check the screen, pick up.

"Thomas!" I say. "Just the man I was thinking of. I was about to call."

"Yeah?"

"Yeah. You'll never guess who offered me a gig."

"Spill."

"Oscar."

"No?" A beat. "Oscar Crumley?"

"Yep."

I know just the mention of the name makes him sweat. Even years later, he hasn't gotten over it.

"Why'd he come see you?"

I give a half-grin he can't see. "That's between him and me."

"Fine, whatever, Mr. Private Eye. Just picturing that asshole ruins my afternoon. And you said yes even though he sent you to prison?"

"You know, guys like me got rent to pay. Our daddies don't foot the bill."

"Quit it."

Thomas is the son of one of the richest men in France—an entrepreneur who in just under thirty years has carved out an empire in construction. He's also my closest friend from college. I can't remember how we became buddies anymore. I think he more or less matched up with the image of the kind of guy I wanted to be back then, when I'd finally leave Belleville far behind and spend my days luxuriating in Passy—like there'd ever be anything for me to do there besides beg for scraps. I vividly remember the first time we ran into Nathalie, without a doubt the hottest girl in the whole school. Also vivid is the memory of seeing Thomas kiss Nathalie right in front of me during a party at someone's town house in the Seventh. Wild with rage, I'd left the festivities, smashing a mirror on my way out. I still have a tiny scar on my left hand from that rush of bogus violence, fitting for a teen with masculinity issues. Thomas and Nathalie started going out. He didn't know she was also sleeping with Oscar Crumley, and two or three other guys, more or less regularly. Since Thomas had no balls, he'd paid me to do his dirty work for him. No balls, but he had brains—probably more useful. I got into trouble, and he married the girl. End of story. Maybe because of this, he has never given up on our friendship, though I suspect he wants to sometimes. For me, just seeing Nat softens any lingering misgivings I have with Thomas.

"Wanted to invite you over for dinner."

"When?"

"Tonight."

"Kind of short notice, isn't it?"

"What, I need to book you two weeks in advance now? If you're busy, say so." He knows better than I do just how shitty my life is.

"I'll be over at nine, cool?"

"Perfect. See you then—and don't bring anything."

No worries there, I think, and hang up.

"Oh, it's you," my grandmother says, opening the door.

"Well, yeah. I said I'd stop by."

"I thought you wouldn't come." Annoyance fills her eyes, set deep into that wrinkled old face. She is the only one who gets to me. We sit down in the living room where an old tape of Arab prayers is playing, surely purchased at a market in the village back home, volume turned up all the way on a radio that saw me born and will probably see me die.

"Think we could maybe pause it for a minute? I can't hear a word you're saying."

She hits stop on the tape deck.

"Thanks."

She points at a chair by the window. I sit down across from her.

"You giving me the silent treatment?" I ask.

"Why'd you do that last night? At your age! You should be ashamed."

I try to play it fair with her. "I'm sorry. I know I fucked up. I don't know what got into me."

"Well, I do. Prison changed things for you. Made the condition worse."

"Fuck, I haven't had a fit in eight months. It's gone for good. No more condition, I promise!" I sigh and stand up. I should've gone home. *Forget it,* I think. *She's an old woman. Just stay. Say your sorry, ask her to translate some songs.* And then I notice the cassette player and remember the tapes again.

"I have work, gotta run. Great seeing you."

Outside, I've made it all of thirty feet when it starts to rain. I run all the way to Gare de l'Est for some shelter, soaked. I should've apologized, should've just shut up for once and stayed a bit longer at my grandmother's. But she's right. After prison, things changed. I can't stay. An empty taxi goes by. I lift my hand, and it pulls over, tossing up a spray of water that stops just short of my shoes. I get inside.

"Rue de Bretagne. I'll give you directions from there."

He drops me at Thibaut's.

I open the door and call into the apartment: "Anyone home?" No answer. The place is empty. So much the better.

I scan Thibaut's room to see if anything's changed, if there's any trace that he's been by or somebody's been messing around. But the room's in the exact same shape as last time. I pull the file with the cassettes from under the bed. In the closet, I find a gym bag and dump them in. The clacking sound they make inside the bag is kind of ridiculous. For good measure, I pull open the desk drawers and dump their contents in too. I'll sort through it all at home. I rifle through the wardrobe, jeans and jacket pockets. Nothing but used metro tickets. The zipper gets stuck; I force it and catch the skin on my thumb. I swear through my teeth and punch the bag in rage. The cassette cases squeak and clatter, like they're telling me to go fuck myself.

———

Back home, I take off my clothes, put on track pants and a sweatshirt. I sit down on my sofa, the cassettes in my hands. No clue what's on them—not a label, nothing on the cases. I remember the losers we all used to be, back when people bought rap mixes to play on their busted-up old boom boxes with shitty sound—all light-years ago. These things are dead. What are they even fucking doing in a student apartment? More to the point, what would a kid be doing with them? I lie down to clear my head, to chase away the distant worry that this whole affair is more complicated than usual, and the bad feeling that the solution's at the bottom of a pool of shit I really don't want to dive into.

The buzzer for the front door startles me off my ass. I check the wall clock. Eight P.M. I fell asleep on my sofa. I get up in a hurry, press the intercom.

"Yes?"

"Idir?" Some punk's voice I don't recognize.

"Who's this?"

"Tarik sent me."

"OK. Third door on your right."

I buzz him in and hear a guy coming up the stairs fast. He reaches the landing. He's still got his helmet on, the visor pulled down. I wave him in and slam the door behind him. He takes off his helmet, revealing his face: the face of a really young guy who hasn't made the right choices in life but doesn't know it yet.

He sticks a hand in his pants pocket and takes out a brown paper envelope cut lengthwise and sealed with packaging tape. He hands it over.

"You're fast. Thanks."

"Careful with the coke; it's pretty uncut. Tarik told me to warn you."

I smile. "Tell him if some chick ODs, I'll rat on him. And you too."

He looks at me, tense.

"Kidding."

He lets out a sigh of relief. I was right to spell it out.

"Right, I get it. Have a nice day."

Once the delivery boy's gone, I empty the envelope's contents on the coffee table. There are two little plastic vials, one full of coke, the other full of pink crystal powder, plus a dozen pills in a bag whose edges have been heat-sealed with a lighter. I check the clock again. I have to hurry; I'm short on time.

I enter the luxurious apartment in the Sixteenth that Nathalie and Thomas have been living in ever since their marriage.

"Hey, Idir, how's it going? You're the first to arrive. My father's late, as usual."

"Your father? Cool, didn't know he was coming." Thomas looks less than thrilled. I move on. "Your lady here?"

"Yeah, she's in the kitchen. Here, give me your coat."

I leave it with him and walk over to the kitchen. Nathalie's busy chopping vegetables. She's wearing a black dress, perfectly fitted to her slender waist. Her grip on the knife makes the muscles along her arm stand out. She looks up when she hears me come in. She's got too much makeup on, trying to hide the rings under her eyes. I never thought she'd be more beautiful than she'd been as a student. Seeing her now, just past thirty, I know I was wrong.

"Hey, Nat."

She smiles.

"Oh, hey, Idir."

I walk over to kiss her on the cheek. She doesn't drop the knife. A heady aroma of sandalwood from her skin sets off the fantasy of a night too rich for sleep.

"How's it going?" she asks, going back to chopping.

"Good, and you?"

She stops for a moment, stares at the slices she's already cut, and sighs. "Could be better."

I can sense a light-headedness in her eyes, the feeling of not knowing what the hell she's doing here, dicing fucking bell peppers to calm herself down. I try to dispel the bad vibes.

"Smells nice, what you're making," I say just as Thomas rushes into the kitchen.

"C'mon, Idir, let me pour you a whisky."

I follow him out and let his wife, hands down the most beautiful woman in Paris, finish making us dinner, thinking she's the one who should be having a whisky while I'm at the stove.

In the living room, I sit down on a great big beige leather sofa. On the redwood coffee table, two glasses, a bowlful of ice cubes, and an imposing bottle, barely touched. Thomas sees me eyeing it and feels compelled to state, as he fills the glasses, "Balvenie."

"Never heard of it."

"Aged for thirty years, Idir."

"Cool. Why would you bother telling me that? You know I don't give a shit," I joke. "You could pour me Label 5 and I wouldn't mind."

He lets out a nervous little laugh, anything but natural.

"You seem nervous. You OK?" I ask.

"Sure, sure, everything's fine," he replies, rubbing his temples.

"You get into it with your wife again?"

He gives me a serious look. "She has a lover."

"Please. You're not starting with this again—"

"I swear—"

"Fuck, man. You've been saying that for ten years. You're like a goddamn broken record."

He takes a few tiny sips of whisky in silence, then starts right back in. "I can't trust her."

"Got any proof?"

"She's acting...funny."

"Got any proof?"

He scratches his head. "I don't have any proof. I just know."

"Quit it. Quit it right now. I don't want to hear your bullshit anymore."

The doorbell rings.

"Ah, at last." Thomas gets up and goes to the door. I recognize his father's voice in the foyer. I stay seated, alone, for a few minutes—just enough time to toss back the rest of my whisky.

It's been a long time since I've seen Eric. I liked him a lot, back in the day. He had a frankness to him most rich people don't have, especially compared with those born rich, solely concerned as they are with managing the fortune preceding generations had already built up. Eric Vernay had fought hard to get where he was. He had that upstart aspect to him that betrayed his common origins. The kind of guy who'd order steak and fries at a high-end restaurant. He probably played up that side of himself, to show how far he'd come, or to throw people off the scent when it came to business. I wondered how many times competitors had taken Eric for a fool, only to find out later on they'd gotten screwed. And yet to anyone from the street, it was obvious straightaway just how dangerous he was. *Sheitan*, my grandmother would've called him. And she'd have been right. The little guy who'd started out as a humble laborer was now extremely rich. And it hadn't happened by accident. Successes like that didn't happen often in this country, hooked as it is on cultural reproduction and incest among the economic elite. All this made him a man as fearsome as he was friendly.

He came barreling into the living room, all smiles. "Ah, Idir. Pleasure to see you again!"

"Mr. Vernay. What a surprise!"

Still the same scrapper's mug, but slightly older now: square jaw, features softened by lines. An old gentleman who must've known lots of women in his life. He gives my hand an energetic shake. Grip steely as ever. He winks. "What, did you get bashful on me? Call me Eric, please."

"Guess I never did get used to calling you that, Mr. Vernay."

He takes off his coat and hands it to his son, revealing his customary stylish charcoal-gray suit. To go by how his jacket hangs from his chest—big pecs, even bigger shoulders—I'm guessing he's a gym rat, and he's probably jumped a chick or two in the locker room.

Thomas slips back into his role as a host.

"I'll get Nat so we can get started with dinner. Have a seat, Dad. Grab him a glass, won't you, Idir?" he says, pointing out where they're all lined up.

I walk over to the cabinet, grab a whisky glass, and set it down next to mine. I pour one for Eric.

"Ice?" I ask.

"Never." He smiles.

I pour myself another and we sit down side by side on the sofa. He toasts me and we clink glasses, locking gazes like tradition demands.

"How long has it been, son? When was the last time?"

"The wedding. Two years."

I can still remember all those douchebags in bow ties and custom-tailored suits. I had to borrow mine from my father;

it was too big. I anesthetized myself with booze so I wouldn't have to listen to conversations about where to invest in Paris real estate. I held all the guests responsible for my hangover and the liter and a half of Moët I spewed up in my apartment as soon as I stepped in the door.

"Two years already. Time starts flying when you get older. It's terrible. What are you up to?"

"Not much. I do what I can. The crisis and all that, am I right? How about you? How's business?"

"Oh, it's tricky for us too these days."

When I think that his company must make several billion a year, I have a hard time believing things are tough for people like him. But figures don't mean a thing anymore, and nobody really knows what goes on in boardrooms. But then, I turned my back on that world a long time ago. It's not that I think poor people are better than rich people. They just have other things on their mind.

"Uneasy lies the head," I say, smiling.

He bursts out laughing. "Exactly, uneasy lies the head—and the crown just gets heavier with age."

We hear voices rising from the kitchen. They must be having a fight for a change. Guess I'm just not lucky with dinners these days. I should think about turning down a few invitations.

"It'll never change," Eric says, and sighs.

A few minutes later, Thomas and Nathalie show up like nothing's wrong. We sit down at the table and start eating. Thomas is strung tight, doesn't talk much, drinks—drinks a lot. But everything goes well, tongues loosen, and I let them right their little world, adding a personal touch now and then. Until it all goes off the rails.

"Nat, you'll never guess who Idir's working for right now."

I hate being put on the spot, especially by my friends. I like being left alone, and public scandals make me uncomfortable. But I realize humiliating me isn't my friend's objective.

"She probably couldn't care less," I say, hoping he'll drop it and move on to something else.

But he presses on tactlessly. "No, tell her—it'll bring back good memories."

"Is this really necessary?"

"He's working for Oscar. Oscar fucking Crumley!" he says triumphantly.

"Really," Eric says, rolling his eyes, "you bring this up over dinner?"

"Remember? The guy who used to fuck you when we were first seeing each other."

With all the calm in the world, Nathalie sets her silverware down beside her plate and leaves the table.

"That's right, leave," he shouts after her as she heads for the stairs.

Eric stares at his son in dismay, but I speak. I can't help myself. "Seriously, why do you do this? Making a spectacle of yourself doesn't help things—"

"Are you defending her?" he asks me fiercely.

"What did you expect her to do?" I say. "You practically called her a whore right in front of us!"

"You just don't get it." Thomas sighs, looking away.

He tosses off the rest of his wine, gets up, and heads for the stairs, going after his wife. I find myself alone at the table with Eric.

"I told him not to marry a woman that beautiful. You're just asking for trouble."

I smirk at Eric's bullshit. "You think he should've picked someone ugly, just for some peace of mind?"

But he doesn't feel like having a laugh. "I've never understood why you stayed friends with him. It's his fault you—"

I cut him off. Don't want to talk about it. "It was my fault. If I hadn't been as dumb, I wouldn't have done it."

"I grew up in a working-class neighborhood too—"

I don't like the way this conversation is going. A guy like him never opens up to anyone unless he's after something. "Let me stop you right there. I may be brown, Monsieur Vernay, but my father's a doctor."

"You misunderstand. I know what it's like to want to be part of a world you don't belong to—what you're willing to do to get there. If my son hadn't been a coward, he would've settled his affairs himself; he wouldn't have paid his best friend, with *my* money, to do it instead."

"What difference does it make?" I ask him curtly. I take a gulp of wine to ease the knot in my throat.

He sets down his cutlery and wipes his mouth slowly with his napkin. "I have a little problem you could maybe help me with."

"I'm listening."

"My chauffeur got assaulted last week. At a red light. A guy in a ski mask stuck a gun under his nose and dragged him out of the car."

"And what exactly do you want?"

"I want the car back."

For the first time in my life, I wonder if Eric is stupid. "Did you file a police report?"

"No," he says, "my wife wanted to, but I told her it was pointless."

"The only problem is if the little shit who stole the car crashes it into the roll-up door at a jewelry store, you'll have to explain to the cops why you never reported it stolen."

"That's my problem."

I get that he doesn't want to discuss his choices. Which means he's got something up his sleeve. "What makes you think I can find your car on my own?"

"I have faith in you."

"Is it an old car? I mean, vintage?"

"No."

"Aren't you insured against theft?"

"Nope."

Impossible, but I let it slide. "In that case," I suggest, "buy another car and report that one stolen. I sincerely believe that to be your best option."

He takes my smile the wrong way. "What's so funny?"

"Look, with your permission, I'm going to be frank. Your car gets jacked, you have to play the game and report it stolen. And you haven't. That's number one."

He frowns.

"Which brings me to number two. What was in the car?"

He is silent.

"If I'm going to work for you, you have to be straight with me. You won't report it stolen, but you want it back. Fine. I just want to ask you one question. Was there something in the car I don't know about right now? Something you don't want to fall into the hands of the police? If so, I have to know. Otherwise, I'll have to turn down your offer."

It's his turn to grin. "You've been watching too many movies, my boy. There's nothing in the car. I just want to be sure I get it back. Let's say it has...sentimental value."

"What leads you to believe your car wasn't stolen by professionals?"

"Nothing about these guys was even remotely *professional*." He stresses the word to show he's doing the explaining. No matter the field, I'm an amateur. "I may be an old man, true— but you don't get rich turning the other cheek. No one steals from me and gets away with it. Not many are even crazy enough to try."

In that case, why ask me to find it, if he's got his own security force? I keep the thought to myself. "How do I go about finding your car? Thefts like that happen every week in Paris by the dozen, and the cars get sold off right after."

"It's an R8," he says in reply, like that's all I need. When I don't react, he adds, "V10."

I decide to clear things up, even if it means my ignorance about cars might be taken as an obvious lack of manliness. "Sorry, this will probably seem weird to you, but I don't know a thing about cars."

"You know what an Audi is?"

"Rings a bell."

"It's their most expensive model."

"Got a big trunk?"

"No, it's a two-seater."

Perfect. Can't load it up, so no way it'll get sold off to run drugs in from the Costa del Sol. No dealers, only private buyers. If it's pricey and eye-catching, the thief will need time to fence it.

"Where did it happen?"

"Near Porte de Pantin."

"Exactly how long ago?"

"Six days."

"Can I talk to your driver?"

He gives me a look with his reptilian eyes. "I'm afraid that won't be possible."

"What did he say the guy looked like?"

"He was young. The usual, but white. According to my chauffeur, that is."

"Young and white—he got all that through a ski mask?"

He shrugs, unimpressed. "That's what he said. Certain things don't get hidden by a mask I guess."

Which means everything and nothing, but just like last time, I let it slide.

"OK, I'll see what I can do. About my fee—"

He cuts me off with a broad wave of his hand. "I'll give you a third of what the car's worth."

I gulp despite myself. That must be a lot. He extends a hand across the table. I shake it for the second time that night. I don't like this hypocrite way of sealing a deal. As if it really meant anything. But after all, the client is king. I decide to get my vengeance in my own way.

"That's what this was all about? Getting me to do a job for you?" I still haven't let go of his hand. He smiles.

"Why, no, my boy. It was just such a great pleasure to see you again."

"Of course," I reply, staring him right in the eyes.

He digs into his jacket pocket and comes up with a business card and a pen. He scribbles something on the back and hands it over. "If you find the car or the guys that stole it, call this number. It's a guy that works for me. He'll take care of everything."

I slip the card into the pocket of my jeans. "Guess I'll be going then. Say bye to Thomas for me, and thank him for dinner."

"Wait, I'll go fetch him."

"No, no, don't bother. They're probably having it out."

No point insisting. Eric's already on his feet and heading upstairs. I get up too and grab my coat from the foyer. I wait a few minutes, eyeing a hideous painting in the hallway. Like the guy who did it squeezed a bunch of colors down his throat and threw them all back up on the canvas. To think I'd have to bust ass for twenty years to afford a piece of shit like that.

Thomas finally comes down and apologizes for the "peculiar" dinner.

"Don't sweat it, man. I'm used to it."

I've got one hand on the door when he holds me back, whispers: "Idir, I'm going to New York for a few weeks. While I'm away, you think you could—"

"No." I cut him off coldly. "If you were going to ask me to follow her, let's just forget we ever had this conversation, and you let me go home in peace with fond memories of a pleasant evening."

"I'll pay. A lot."

"What part of 'no' did you not understand? You're the only one who hasn't changed; you're the same shithead you always were."

Offended, he retorts, "You think you're better than me?"

This time, I open the door. "Take some time off, buddy. Thanks for dinner."

CHAPTER 2

TEN A.M. THE ACID TASTE IN MY MOUTH MAKES ME WANT TO keep sleeping. I get up around noon with a slight headache that just won't go away, even after two aspirins. I didn't think I'd boozed it up that much last night. I thought wrong.

I take the metro to Belleville for my weekly lunch with Cherif. I've known him ever since we were kids. A buddy from the neighborhood I met at school. He liked me a lot; I did his homework for him. Suited me just fine. In return, he defended me from bullies and kept me from getting beaten up. I think that's how our friendship got started. While I was taking my *baccalauréat* to get into college, he was already one of the most notorious thieves in the capital. It began with mopeds. He'd borrow one for a joyride around the neighborhood, then put it back a little farther down the boulevard. Plus he had a way with anything on wheels. A goddamned gift. Even as a teen, Cherif could jump a three-hundred-pound CBR and steer it like a razor scooter. The local crews spotted him fast. The first thing he drove for them were lead cars on drug runs to Mokum and back, then carry cars—the overland equivalent of a cigarette boat. All with no license, since he wasn't even old enough. Legend has it that once at a Belgian highway roadblock on the way back, he flipped a bitch and returned to Paris by way of Germany, Austria, and Italy. I've never asked him if it was true.

Even if it was, he'd tell me it wasn't with the slightest of crooked smiles, the kind you let slip to make doubt linger. He'd stopped driving and begun focusing on carjacking. "No violence," he likes to specify even now, always joking, "I'm the Kabyle Arsène Lupin, gentleman thief."

But behind this juvenile trash talk lay the truth. Cherif was the only one who didn't jack cars by threatening drivers with guns or Tasers, or beating them with a helmet. Modern security systems on vehicles, especially high-end ones, had driven thieves to target drivers rather than ignition switches. But Cherif was old school. If he laid hands on anything, it was going to be the car. As far as I knew, he was the only one who still worked like that.

We'd fallen out of touch over the years, and then gotten back in touch when I was in the pen. I don't know how he found out. We hadn't spoken for two or three years and then suddenly, there he was, having a conversation with me like nothing had happened. Six months for a guy like him was nothing. But he knew it was a lot for me, and he wanted to make sure I had everything I needed.

The heat on the boulevard is almost unbearable. Café terraces full of hipsters, attentive to the slightest ray of sunshine. No doubt about it, the neighborhood where I grew up has changed. I climb rue de Belleville, shirt sticking to my back with sweat, all the way to the restaurant where we're supposed to meet. We've been meeting up for lunch once a week for years now, ever since I got out. Cherif's waiting outside—short jacket, shaved skull, trimmed beard, and a smile on his face, as usual. We go inside the packed restaurant. The not-very-friendly waiter seats us at a tiny table by a young couple dressed like artists, who are forced to move their chairs so we can sit down.

"Why is it like this now?" Cherif complains, darting glances at the people around us.

"No idea. It's *Madame Rosa* syndrome. What these people don't get is that story's fun to watch but hard to live. And it was before the euro, racial tensions between communities, and all that shit."

"*Madame Rosa*—that's the book with the Jew and the whore you lent me?" Cherif asks, who could give a shit about my theories and is just checking to see that his memory still works.

"He wasn't Jewish. He was a second-generation North African. The whore was the one who was Jewish."

Cherif scowls. He doesn't give a shit; it's all the same to him. All he wants is to get the reference I'm making.

"Yeah, it was a fun book. So, how's business?"

"All right."

He does a double take. "Damn, this is a first."

"What?"

"Where's all the pissing and moaning about no work, shit work, et cetera?"

"I've got two cases. It's actually kind of busy."

"Are you kidding? Wait, call the waiter, we're having champagne!" He lifts his hand and calls over the guy who seated us. "*Garçon! Garçon!*"

The waiter turns and starts heading over. I pull Cherif's hand down. "Cut the bullshit!"

I wave the waiter away. He shrugs and heads off again.

Cherif is laughing. "C'mon, dude, don't be like that! But seriously, that's amazing. Spill."

"I have to find a kid who ran away and recover a stolen ride." I pause a moment. "Say, you know anything about cars?"

He bursts out laughing again. "Shithead."

"I have to find one for this guy. It got carjacked by Porte de Pantin."

"So what? Happens all the time. What was he thinking?"

"Apparently it's a pretty sweet ride, an R8."

He almost chokes. "An R8?"

"Yeah. Vio," I add, hoping I'm getting the digits right.

"An R8—damn, who you working for?"

"A guy who wants to find his car."

"You know a piece of shit like that's worth at least 150,000 euros, right?"

My mouth drops with this unexpected news. I wasn't expecting that much. A third of that is...I really have to start asking more questions.

"You think you could help me get it back?" I ask Cherif. "Find out who lifted it? A car like that doesn't just go by unnoticed."

"That's for sure. Whoever took it'll have a hard time fencing it. I can put the word out you're interested, for ten grand."

"Five?" I haggle, watching my cut go down.

He shakes his head. "With ten, you're sure to have a name in some suburb of the City of Lights before the car disappears."

"OK, fine."

"Plus, I'm sure that given your client, ten big ones won't feel like a thing."

I suppress a grin. He's full of surprises.

"I knew it! Damn, you're lucky I make a good living. You would've spread the wealth at least?"

"Oh, sure."

We both burst out laughing.

"Asshole! You wouldn't have given me a red cent!"

I pay for lunch.

"Where are you headed? Home?"

"No, I'm headed over to Bes-bar."

_____

Barbès. A thousand strains of Arabic fill your ears, from Egyptian—the pure stuff—to the backwoods Maghreb lingo most kids speak. A store, one of many on the boulevard, anarchy inside and no AC, just an old fan spinning slo-mo; a bazaar where anyone can find anything used and in decent shape, more or less. Fifteen minutes of elbowing to rummage through the bins of piled-up discards until I finally find what I'm looking for: an old-school Sony Walkman, battery operated. I walk out of the shop dripping sweat, feeling like I've won a battle against dust and time.

Swing by Franprix for some batteries and now here I am on my sofa, my battered earbuds stuck in my ears. And we're off.

Tape goes by. Nothing. Crackling. I hit the fast-forward button. Scratching sounds that bring me back to the park benches of my adolescence. Then a monotone voice, weak but unyielding:

I made love to her yesterday. Or at least I tried. We'd had a few drinks, she insisted...After all, we're supposed to be going out, right? Knowing her, she probably asked as more of a challenge. I must be the only man she knows who doesn't want to jump her. I forced myself to do it like everyone else, even though they're all worthless...She did everything she could to turn me on without managing to. Only I could do it. When I realized the sooner I finished, the sooner it would all be over, I concentrated on giving her what she wanted, unplugged from the act so I wouldn't feel a thing anymore, freeing myself, free and easy,

*while my mind fled far, far away from the bed. When it was
done, she smiled at me, happy, makeup mixed with sweat on
her cheeks, pleased with herself. She smelled of sweat and sex,
sex for no reason except feeling like a shit afterward. I left her
there and took a long shower. When I went back into the room,
she was gone. I changed the sheets and opened the window. I
shivered, slipping under the sheets. I slept well, the well-earned
sleep of the just...No dreams.*

No music, just confessions. Thibaut's confessions. Not what
I expected. What's a kid like that making tapes for? I eject
the cassette, grab another one at random, and slip it in, torn
between the joy of finding something and the anguish of having to listen to this endless stream of private words until I feel
like throwing up. But I get some answers.

*This is what I've decided to do. Every day, on this old tape
player. Record myself. That's not right. It's more like I'm telling
myself about stuff and recording my voice. Writing it down
would be cheating. There's a filter: time to think, to censor, to
hide from ridicule or even dramatize it. There's nothing here.
Nothing but me. I never go back, never listen to it again—few
people like themselves so much they can stand hearing their
own voice. I hate myself enough not to be one of those people.
At least this makes me talk—otherwise, all this stuff would stay
buried. The whole point is just to get it out, not to be heard.
I don't want anyone's pity. I just want to be free—to empty
myself out and stay empty.*

She's right across from me, on the sidewalk, with three other stupid but still pretty party girls holding their cigarettes like paintbrushes.

"Eve?"

Not very happy to see me, she mumbles, "Hey."

Her friends shoot me dirty looks.

"Can I talk to you for a second?"

She catches on quick that I'm not giving her a choice, that I'll just keep standing right by their table like a real prick, ready to stomach all their chitchat about guys and fashion. She gets up, tells her friends she won't be long. We walk a few yards away, and she takes a nervous drag of her cigarette without looking at me.

"How'd you find me?"

"I asked Charles."

"Did you have to?"

"If you'd told me everything right from the start, and answered your phone, you could've been sipping your Chablis in peace."

"Look, I told you everything—"

"You weren't going out. Don't bother lying, there's no point. I get that women weren't really his thing." I don't need to tell her about the tapes and that time they fucked; she doesn't ask any questions. For the first time she seems sad, genuinely concerned by what I'm telling her.

"We were never really going out, we were just friends." With a long drag, she finishes her cigarette and tosses it in the gutter. "We had a kind of arrangement. I was supposed to pretend to be his girlfriend at school, with his father—"

She stops, swallows.

"There it is," she says with a sigh of relief.

"So if I'm getting you right, his college friends and his family didn't appreciate it, right?"

She nods.

"What a shitty crowd, huh?"

"Yeah."

"You know the men he saw?"

"No."

"Never ran into one?"

"No, he's very secretive about who he sees. He's a brilliant guy, but self-conscious, discreet. I like him a lot."

"How about at school?"

"Not that I know of. He didn't want to see guys from his own crowd."

"By choice or from fear it would get around?"

She shrugs. "Both. I don't know."

"All right. You really don't know anything else? Where he'd go when he wasn't pretending to be someone else? Think."

"Once we went to eat by the Opéra. He was nervous. I asked him what was wrong. He had to go to a special party afterward, find a friend of his in the neighborhood. It seemed to make him nervous. That's the only time he ever mentioned anyone, but no names."

"And afterward?"

"Nothing. He walked me to a taxi stand and left for his party."

"He say where he was going?"

"No."

"OK. Sorry to bother you. In the future, try not to hide stuff like this from me anymore. Please?"

She nods, a sad little girl all of a sudden, taking another cigarette out of her pack and sticking it in her mouth.

"I'll see you tomorrow, for the party. Go on back to your friends."

Only once I've crossed the street do I turn around and realize she hasn't moved, her unlit cigarette still stuck to her lips.

I go back home. The Walkman's still there on the sofa. With paper, pen, and a roll of Scotch tape, I number the cassettes. Then I run them through the player on fast-forward, trying to sift out facts—names, dates, places—from more general confessions.

I've decided to not talk about people specifically, not channel my hatred at anyone, just talk about my experiences, my feelings, to draw lessons from the man, or rather the creature, I am...

I spend an hour listening to him talk about his life, his family, his studies, and other bullshit.

He invited me to the party. I said yes. I felt frightened right away. He was a sadistic guy, you could tell just by looking. But I resolved to forget my fear. I'm afraid shame sets it off. I've decided not to feel any more guilt about what I am. I've known all my life, and sometimes I saw my father and brother do disgusting things. I don't care about their morality; I want to puke it up till it's all gone from my stomach, even if I have to stick my fingers all the way down my own throat...So I said yes and I even felt a twinge of arousal as I did so. I'll go to the party without a thought in my head...except for my own pleasure. For the first time.

His voice changes, becomes hesitant, laden with sobs.

I had dinner with Eve before heading over. She could tell I was stressed out. He gave me no choice. I'm ashamed to say I was turned on before it all happened. He was handsome and attractive. When he forced himself on me, he joined that long line of men polluting my family and the world, men who think only in terms of power and submission, incapable of understanding anything except the logic of the most brutal action. They're vulgar monsters, as horrible as they are horribly banal... The same things make them hard, the same hatred drives them, the same boundless narcissism, the same taste for perversion and harassment. I was ashamed when the bartender found me and asked if I wanted him to call the police. I saw myself having to explain it all to men in uniform, to the authorities, starting with my lifelong disgust all the way to the abyss of tonight. I told him not to do anything. I was a coward. I decided to stay silent...I went home and stayed there in the dark...

The sign sizzles. I hope this is the place. I've been to four gay bars so far, showing around photos of the kid. Everywhere, guys shake their heads. They seem sincere; none of them bat an eyelid when they see the photo, and they all agree to contact me without asking for ID or anything. No trace of Thibaut. Starting to feel a little trashed because I've bought at least a drink each time, so as not to be that asshole who asks questions and never gives anything back. I figure if I'm going to play cop, I don't have to play the stingy one.

I stop in front of the metal door, vowing that if no one here's ever heard of him, I'll call it a night. The thought of my own bed fills me with joyful anticipation, and I'm almost sorry the guy eyeing me through the peephole decides to open up. Square jaw, short blond hair stiff with gel. He's got a cheap suit on, the seams about to burst. A real minotaur. A wee light goes on in my head. If this goes south, I'll need to run, because short of a gun, there's no way I'm getting the better of this guy.

I forget the bouncer and head down the stairway underground. It's a small club, the music all the way up. For the first time that night, I feel like I'm in a William Friedkin movie. All old-timers, guys pushing fifty, built like moving men with dinged-up faces. They're all eyeing me when I walk in. A bar, a tiny dance floor, and a few sagging sofas. It smells like sweat and other things I don't want to think about. I act like I don't notice a thing, sit at the bar, and flag down a bartender wearing a leather vest and denim shorts.

"Whisky, please."

He gives me my whisky. "Ten euros."

I pay, take a first sip, set my glass down on the counter. I check out the room; no one's looking my way anymore. Lots of drinking, two couples slow dancing and making out on the floor. I turn back toward the bartender and show him Thibaut's photo.

"Ever seen him before?"

"No," he says, lowering his eyes.

"At least take a look at the photo."

The bartender acts like he doesn't understand and starts racking the clean glasses behind him. I've been at this for three and a half hours. I'm sick of playing detective, sick of this shitty evening. "Hey! I'm talking to you! You know this guy or not?"

"I don't have to answer your questions, and you've got no fucking business here. So beat it," he hisses.

I give him a smile. "I paid for my drink. And guess what? I like it here. I'm in no hurry..."

The bartender disappears through a door behind the bar. I have just enough time to swipe a corkscrew from behind the counter and stick it in my jacket pocket before he shows up again, baseball bat in hand. He winds up, ready to take a swing at my head. I get up from the stool, hands in the air.

"Hey, it's cool! It's cool!"

"I said get the fuck out."

"OK, OK! I'm going!" When I turn around, the goliath from the entrance is right behind me. He grabs me by the collar, drags me upstairs, and throws me out. My feet scrape asphalt for several yards before I get my balance back.

———————

I check my watch. One A.M.

I'm bored with waiting here watching the doorway, back stiff against the gates of the Palais Royal gardens, but I'd rather settle this tonight. *Without your baseball bat and your buddy, you won't be such a smart little bastard.* To kill time, I try to figure out what movie that club reminds me of. I can't remember. Shit, Pacino was in it. Goddamn memory. I nod off against the gates.

I wake to the voices of clientele exiting the club drunk. They all walk right by without paying me the slightest mind, like I'm a beggar spending a mild night under the stars.

It takes another quarter hour of cooling my heels and blowing on my hands before the bartender closes up. The bouncer sticks close and they talk in low voices. I hope they'll split up, but alas, they keep walking side by side. This is looking harder than I imagined. I let them get a good dozen yards ahead of me and then stand up, corkscrew in hand. I've never attacked anyone with a corkscrew before, but I figure a shiv is a shiv, even a twisted one. It'll work as long as the handle stays on.

I start running after them. The sound of my footsteps tips off the bouncer, who turns. Too late. I plant the corkscrew right in his crotch and yank my arm up to be sure I've pierced flesh. I let go of the weapon, and he crumples, howling. I smack the bartender, a glancing blow in the jaw, and turn back to the bouncer. He's screaming, holding his balls. With one quick stroke, I pull the corkscrew out. I've rarely heard a man scream this loud; he'll probably be unconscious soon. The barman tries to get away but, still dazed from the blow, he's not going very fast. I catch up to him a dozen yards away, slamming him against a car. I hold the corkscrew over his cheekbone.

"The guy in the photo! Tell me what you know, or I'll scrape your eye out."

He gulps. I tighten my hold on his jacket collar with my left hand. "I swear I'll do it."

His words are broken by sobs. "He just came once. A regular brought him in. I don't know how they knew each other. He didn't like the atmosphere, he was uncomfortable—he didn't expect—"

"What happened?"

"He didn't give the kid a choice."

"Who?"

"The guy, he dragged him to the toilets and locked them in. Fifteen minutes later, he hightailed it out of there. I found the kid in tears inside, pants around his ankles. He was bleeding. I asked if he wanted me to call the cops. He said no. So I helped him get dressed, and he left."

I picture the kid, cornered, getting raped by a degenerate in the bathroom when all he wanted was to have a drink and do some flirting. "The guy—what's his name?"

"I don't know."

"Don't you fuck with me."

"I swear! I don't really know him. We shot a movie together, for a guy who does really special stuff. No one ever uses their real name. We all use aliases. Calls himself Tantalus."

"What kind of stuff?"

"Not the kind you watch at home on Saturday night! Let me go! I told you everything I know."

I keep him there for a few more seconds, staring into his eyes to make sure he's not lying.

"I swear!"

I hear a siren in the distance. I let him go and start running down the street. Once I'm on the boulevards, I slow down. I wipe the corkscrew with a handkerchief and toss it in a trash can.

Back home, chilled to the bone, I find myself sitting in front of a cup of coffee, sobbing like a kid till my nose runs.

One of my mysterious crying jags. It's not related to stress, depression, or anything like that. It can happen at any time and just double me over. It's always been like this. The various shrinks I saw as a kid said it had to do with my mother leaving. The doctor in prison explained they were attacks of claustrophobia, because I couldn't stand being locked up. And you know what my grandmother says. All I know is it's never gone away for more than a few months at a time. It always comes back, completely disconnected from the reality of the moment, never anything to do with how I feel. I could be on a beach in the Caribbean with a Russian model lying next to me, and I'd still be blubbering salty tears into my mojito. It's pretty embarrassing, but I've learned to live with it.

CHAPTER 3

I WAKE UP ON MY SOFA, STILL DRESSED. IT HURTS TO SWALLOW; caught a cold staking out the club. I reheat old coffee and go over what I've learned. Thibaut had gone to that club only once. I suspected as much: the place didn't exactly fit his profile. The guy who took him there put him through hell. Slim chance it was premeditated. Why drag someone to a public place just to assault him? Whoever did it must have been unable to control his urges. Just one thought about what that baby went through and my nerves start fraying. Powerless. Tantalus: a bullshit stage name isn't much to go on. I wonder if the guy could've killed Thibaut. Crime of passion, or fear his victim would press charges? Right now I don't know much more, so I just try to convince myself of one thing: Paris is a small town, and I'll catch the bastard.

In the neighborhood, morning is drawing to a close. The sun is shining, and watching the comings and goings from the sex shops, I think these guys must really be motivated to rub one out in the middle of the day. I join them, pass Pigalle, and duck into the only boutique I know nearby. Inside, a guy is reading plot synopses on the backs of boxes, like a true movie lover. I go down to the basement, with its row of peep show booths. Behind the counter, a punkette with dyed red hair and a nose piercing is flipping through a women's magazine that looks downright cheery. Her eyes perk up when she sees me coming.

"Hey, friend. What's your pleasure?"

"Uh..."

She starts in with her sales pitch, reciting from the catalog. "How about a lesbian show for ten eur—"

"Thanks, but no thanks."

"OK then, guy-girl show upstairs. Starts in about fifteen minutes."

"I'm here to see Moshe."

She gives me a weird look. "You a friend?"

"You could say that."

She goes through a door behind her, leaving me alone for a few seconds among the skin flicks, the dildos, the latex masks. Spotting an inflatable goat in the window display, I have to smile.

"I cannot fucking believe it!"

I turn around. Short, squat. Same old yarmulke on his head, same old Jewish gangster's mug and the manners to go with. Moshe is orthodox, very serious when it comes to religion. Which doesn't keep him from running a good dozen sex shops all over Paris. I've known him since I was ten and he kept a store owner at the Marché Cadet from smashing a crate over my head for pinching a few items. Moshe bought me a coffee and we'd played cards all day.

"You better fucking believe it!" I open my arms, and we give each other a hug.

"Is it really you? How's it going?"

"All right. You?"

"*Baruch Hashem*, I'm well. Back when you lived in Belleville, you used to cross town to come see me, I shit you not. Now you live right next door, and you never come around."

"Oh, cut it out." I point at the plastic goat. "Are there really guys who buy that?"

"Of course." He shrugs. "You want one, I'll give you a good price for it."

He winks, and I grin. "Moshe, I need some information."

"I'm listening."

I lower my voice. "I'm looking for a guy who does porno videos, mostly gay stuff, probably, though he might do a bit of everything."

"There are lots of guys like that."

"I figured, but I don't really know much about him. All I know is his stage name. Calls himself Tantalus."

"I know a guy who could help you out. He makes movies." He picks up a phone on the counter and dials a number. "Yeah... Adrian there? You know what time he'll be back? OK, thanks." He hangs up. "He's not in yet, should be about an hour or so. You eat yet?"

I shake my head.

"Then come with me," he says, grabbing his coat from behind the counter. "My treat. We'll go see Adrian together after."

We head down toward the Grands Boulevards and end up in a little Tunisian place right by the Folies Bergère. Once we order, Moshe takes a small cigar from his jacket pocket.

"I come here because it's the only place in the neighborhood where they let me smoke now." He lights up and takes little puffs. "So why do you need to know all this? Thinking of getting into the movies?" he teases.

"I have to find a kid. Never fit in among his own people. Probably rejected because of his sexual orientation. A good kid, but fragile, wound up going out with some real bastards. I know this guy hung around him. Definitely did some things to him."

"Like?"

"Like fucked-up shit."

"Poor kid."

After lunch, the owner serves us up some brandies, and we head back toward Pigalle. Moshe briefs me about the guy we're going to see.

"I'm warning you right now, he's no friend of mine. I can't stand him. But if anyone can help you, it's him."

We walk down boulevard de Clichy until Moshe stops in front of a sex shop, as if picking one at random from the legion along the sidewalk. Pushing aside a heavy curtain of ocher fabric, he goes in. I follow. It looks just like all the others inside: weak neon lighting, movies everywhere, booths to the left. There's a lost-looking kid minding the store: double chin poorly shaved, *Star Wars* tee, a tiny pair of glasses perched on the end of his nose.

"Adrian here?" Moshe asks.

The kid nods, picks up the phone, mutters something, and hangs up. "You're good, he's up top. He's shooting right now, but you can go up." He points at a spiral iron staircase way at the back of the room.

I fall in step behind Moshe. I can hear pop music now—1980s shit, complete with revolting synth. The staircase leads to what looks like a small theater with rows of seats and a stage bathed in harsh light. A guy with a camera is sitting up front, barking directions at two tall, exceptionally athletic women fondling each other and kissing to the music. Even from a distance, the show is pathetic. As usual.

"That him?" I ask Moshe.

"Yeah."

Moshe walks over and calls out to him. "Working hard?"

The man turns around. "Moshe. It's been a while."

He turns to the models. "All right, get dressed, girls. Take a break. Be back in fifteen."

As they prance by us, I realize the girls are in fact guys dressed up with wigs and sequined dresses—pop star look-alikes. One of them has an Adam's apple twice the size of mine and looks like a popular platinum-blond singer.

Moshe introduces me. "This is Idir. A good friend of mine."

Adrian extends his hand. I look him right in the eyes. He's an ash blond with a high forehead, bulging eyes, and a tiny debauched mouth. The kind of guy no girl would want to see entering her subway car late one Saturday night.

"Pleasure," he says.

I shake his hand. It's soft through and through.

"Well, I doubt this is a social call. Not that it doesn't delight me to see you, but I've got work," says Adrian.

"We'd like some information about an actor."

I take over. "A guy who dabbles now and then, amateur stuff. I think he's bi. Calls himself Tantalus."

Adrian looks at me, annoyed. "Look, guys, I make movies, but this isn't Hollywood here. I pay cash, and nobody's giving me an invoice. The people who come here, we're not talking cream of the crop. We make up names for the credits—whatever sounds funniest when we're editing, that's all. Sorry, can't help you. Other producers, guaranteed, they'll tell you the same thing. You're wasting your time."

I walk Moshe back to work and thank him for his help. Back at my place, I make myself more coffee, settle down on the couch, and feel the tears coming, unprovoked. I cry for two hours before it goes away. Flat on my back till evening, just hoping it will pass. The problem with the crying jags is they aren't just about what happens during. There's also what happens after. I lose time, I never know how much. In the dark, the veins in my neck ready to explode, I'm huffing like a bull after a charge, sucking my salty tongue.

Around eight, my hands finally stop trembling. My tear ducts dry up. I can do what I have to do.

––––––––––––––

The apartment building rises from one of those narrow perpendicular streets off boulevard Saint-Germain. I pull out my phone, check Eve's text message, and punch in the security code. The first door opens. I walk a few yards and run into another, by the concierge's quarters. I scan the intercom by last name and buzz up.

The elevator is about the size of my kitchen. I reach the sixth floor. Just one door on the landing, cracked open. I freeze on the threshold and push the door slowly open with an elbow, careful not to touch the jamb with my fingers.

The apartment is dimly lit, the foyer huge. I cross on tiptoe. "Eve?"

No answer. A light is on in a room somewhere. A bedroom. From the hallway, I see the foot of a bed. A muddled sound of objects clanking, like someone's searching the place. I do an about-face for the front door and grab a candlestick from a buffet heavy enough to do the job. I feel better about my chances now.

The bedroom. A king-size bed bracketed by shelves full of books. An en suite bath. That's where the sounds are coming from. In front of a mirror, wearing nothing but a black G-string, Eve is applying her makeup, her ass on display like it's nothing, like she thinks asses that perfect are a regular sight for guys like me. When she reaches out to grab her mascara from a shelf, the arch of her back makes a long arabesque.

"Sorry, I'm not ready yet," she says, glancing at me in the mirror.

"I thought—I'll, uh, just wait outside." I chuck the candlestick on the bed, hold my hand out right in front of me. It's trembling.

"You OK?" she asks innocently.

"Yeah. Where are we going tonight?"

"To Hugo's."

I don't even know why I asked her such a stupid question. She comes out in a loose top that stops midthigh, her long brown hair swept back in a big chignon. She's wearing jeans tight as a second skin and red heels.

"Ready?" I ask.

But she doesn't seem to want to follow me. Instead, she lies down lubriciously on the bed. "You bring anything?"

Without fanfare, I dismiss the disappointment. *Really, Idir, you can dare to dream—but it'll never happen.* I take the drugs out from under my balls, apologize for how ungentlemanly that is, but honestly, I've never understood people who walk around with their stash in their coat pocket, like there's no such thing as stop and frisk.

"Take your pick."

She sits up and points at the pink powder Tarik gave me. What can I say? My man knows his business. She grabs a DVD off the floor. *Contempt.* It pains me, but I lay a line out for her on the clamshell, thinking her ass is a sure match for Bardot's. She snorts the powder up diligently, no straw, just holding one nostril closed. A real pro.

"Not having any?"

I put the drugs away without answering. "We good to go now?"

She gives a capricious little pout. "I'll call a taxi."

In the elevator, the light from above brings out a slight bruise on her left cheek. Something she could've gotten walking into a door. Once we're in the taxi, I ask her what it's from. She could tell me to go fuck myself, but she replies quite naturally, as if I'd asked her for the time.

"A guy I see now and then. He has these weird fits."

"What do you mean 'weird'? He gets violent?"

"Not really. He's not normally violent, but let's just say he likes violence when…"

"When you fuck," I finish, not very delicately.

She looks at me sideways. "Right. But why are you interested?"

"I don't know. I wonder why a girl like you, who could have any boy she wants, gets herself into these kinds of situations."

"Hasn't it ever occurred to you I could like it?"

"Right on."

She laughs.

"What's so funny?"

"I was thinking about the guy—"

"Who? The guy who hit you?"

"Yeah. He likes it when I hurt him too. When I…penetrate him."

I wonder how far this chick will go. "And?"

"And each time, he starts jabbering about twisted stuff."

"Like what?"

"Like—what was that thing he said last time? Oh, yeah: 'Make me suffer, condemn me to being…condemn me to suffering…' Something like that, I can't even remember. Sick stuff. I was dying laughing."

The phrase echoes in my head, like I've heard it before, somewhere.

"You OK? You look green."

"I'm fine. Your boyfriend just sounds like one special guy. Oh, and listen, at this party: we're friends, OK? I'm your dealer, not your financial adviser."

I spend the rest of the cab ride racking my brain to no avail for what that phrase reminds me of. The taxi drops us in the Seventeenth. I should've asked where the party was; would've saved me crossing Paris twice. The building is very modern. You can hear the bass from the street. Eve taps in the entrance code. The door opens on a large courtyard; at the back are a few apartments whose patios are separated by wooden partitions. There are twenty or so people, beers in hand, having conversations. Eve says her hellos; I hang back and give them a little wave, a kind of collective greeting. They all look at me, intrigued. She tells them something, but I can't hear it, and at once they all relax. I think the most observant have guessed from my milk-chocolate dome that I'm not a regular around here. Eve comes back toward me.

"Let's get something to drink."

We enter the living room through wide-open sliding glass doors. The music's turned all the way up. I follow her to the kitchen, dodging en route a young girl wiggling around by her lonesome. Towering over the bar are stockpiled bottles and plastic cups. As Eve pours herself vodka, I ask, "What'd you tell the people outside?"

"About you? That you were my dealer. Like you asked. What are you having?"

"I'll have a Jack."

She pours, pointing a finger at the soda bottles on the table. "What with? Coke?"

"Straight up," I say, taking the cup from her hand.

We toast. I take a gulp, eyes riveted on the living room, which has become an improvised dance floor where cute girls in short dresses are swaying their hips. Eve asks me if I like what I see.

I smile. "Between friends? I'm too old for that."

"But do you like it, Idir?" This little girl already knows everything about the sexual hang-ups of men in general—and I'm no exception.

"Yeah, they're pretty."

Just then, a boy comes up and starts talking to Eve. Tall, skinny guy, poorly shaven, with a lock of hair falling over his eyes. He seems happy to see her. She feels obliged to introduce us.

"Hugo, our host. Idir, a friend."

"Pleasure," he says.

He seems sincere. Eve must've filled him in. I don't feel like having the two of them underfoot all night just because I'm playing pharmacist.

"Can I offer you a line?"

Eve and the skinny douchebag break out in huge smiles, a display of affection I'm not used to, at least not when it's directed at me. *Tarik, you lucky bastard, people must love you.*

Hugo drags us upstairs. We go into his room; there's a poster for *Pierrot le fou* on his wall. *Damn, what is it with all these kids and Godard?* I turn my back on him, let them snort their shit while staring at Belmondo, his face painted blue. Hugo gets up and declares it's good stuff. He asks if I can score some more easy. I toss him the bag, which he catches midflight, and then I leave the room before I'm overwhelmed by the desire to punch him. I go downstairs to mingle with the other guests. I figure hanging around the bar is a good way of making sure I talk to everyone. So I pour myself another Jack Daniel's and settle in by the bottles, watching the girls dance, like some sad old loser.

A guy who looks like a high school football player straight out of some American TV show bumps into me. He's already pretty tipsy and has to steady himself on the bar for a moment to stay upright. I take no notice. He grabs a beer, uncaps it with his lighter, and takes a long swallow. When he goes by me again, I can't help myself: I stick my foot out. He trips over it and all six feet of him hit the floor. The beer he just grabbed goes rolling away, pouring out its contents. Quick as he went down, he's back on his feet, eyes wide and alert, as if the fall sobered him up. Furious, he points a finger at me, and shouts, "Fuck you do that for?"

I look at him evenly and, without raising my voice, say, "I didn't do anything, man. You're the one who's drunk and can't stand up straight."

He pulls his fist back, but his friends pop up out of nowhere and surround him. They move him away, trying to calm him down. Never punch the drug dealer. He's still struggling and shouting insults at me, wild with rage. Just then, Eve shows up. I didn't know she'd watched the whole scene. I give her a smile.

"Drop it," she says.

"Oh, I wasn't about to get all worked up." I eye her lips a little too intently. I don't think she'd care if I eyed her intently all night. As long as I was the one with the drugs.

"Ignore him. I told you the guy was weird."

I look at her, smiling. "So he's Tantalus?"

She gives me a weird look. "What? No, he's the guy I told you about on the way over."

I should drink more often. Sometimes connections get made without my even realizing. I'd call it genius if it hadn't taken me so long. Which makes me a dumb fuck instead. I forget that I've been to college, am capable of logical reasoning, can do something besides this shitty job where I'm paid under the table.

"'Condemned to thirst forever'—is that what you said to me in the taxi?" I ask her, taking a firm grip on her arm.

"Yeah—I mean, I don't remember. Something like that."

Tantalus. Torment. I must look like a visionary right now, or a crank. Thank you, Dad, for keeping me from spending my days in the streets and forcing me to go to class. What a dumb fuck I was. Why couldn't the guy who'd taken Thibaut to the club also be one of his friends?

"What's his name?"

"Who?" she asks.

"The guy I just messed with."

"Julien."

"He do drugs?"

"Does he ever," she replies, with a smile that tells me that if he were a blue-collar boy, she'd call him a junkie.

"Perfect. Go see him. Tell him I want a word. Say I'm ready to give him a little pick-me-up as an apology."

She stares at me, eyes wide open.

"Stop staring at me like that. C'mon now, please?"

She obeys. I knock off the rest of my glass and follow her out on the patio. I look around for her. She's holding Julien's hand in a corner of the yard. I walk over to them and extend my hand. "Try this again? I'm Idir."

He looks me over warily without replying or taking my hand. I figure it's time for the pills to come out. I don't know what the fuck they are, but he pops two like they're candy before I can even ask if he wants any.

"Keep the rest, if you want. I'm sorry about earlier. It was an accident." Discreetly, I signal Eve to clear off and leave us alone. She gets it and goes. He watches her walk off, eyeing the sway of her hips.

"You fuck her already?" he asks, just like that.

"Nope."

I know guys like him. He wants me to turn the question around so he can say he fucked her, give me all the details of what he did to her, tell me she was screaming with pleasure and begging for more. Guys like him make me want to puke. Instead, I say, "I'm headed out. This party's too tame for me."

"Where to?"

I can feel him on the hook. "Score something. I'm all out."

A spark lights up in his eye. "Any way you could get some for me?"

"Depends. You got cash?"

"Not on me."

"Sorry, man, I don't do credit."

"Can't you get it delivered here? While I go hit up an ATM?"

I shake my head. "My guy won't deliver to a place he doesn't know, especially with tons of people around."

He nods like he understands. I make ready to leave. That's how you win at this game.

"Hey!"

"What?"

"We can wait at my place, if you want. Think he'll go for that?"

"You live alone?"

Outside. We get in his car, a metallic-gray Mini. For ten minutes, give or take, we cross a deserted city, shitty electro music turned all the way up, without exchanging a word. He's too high to talk, staring at the road in front of him, eyes wide open. He's starting to scare me. We reach a carriage entrance a stone's throw from the Champs-Élysées; he pops the door with the beep of an opener. We park at the rear of the building's inner courtyard. He gets out of the car, lets out a mumbled, "Over here," keeps on mumbling to himself. I shouldn't have given this fuckwit all those pills.

He doesn't bother switching on the light, and I follow him up the stairs in the dark. He takes the steps quickly; I lose him and flatten myself against the wall to keep going, for fear of a nasty surprise. On the landing he finally hits the lights. His hand's trembling; he drops his keys. Not a good sign. We enter the apartment. He tosses his coat on the floor and looks at me, white saliva flecking the corners of his mouth.

"You call him now?"

"All right. What's your pleasure?" I pull out my phone.

He sounds like a kid writing Santa a letter. "Uh, two grams of—"

"You know what? I call him, he drops by with whatever he has left, and you take your pick, OK?"

He nods. "OK."

I dial Cherif. He's the guy I trust the most. Or maybe he's the one I'm most comfortable getting in trouble with. He doesn't pick up and it goes to voice mail. I leave him a message with the address, asking him to get back to me as soon as he can. I turn back to Julien. He's staring with glazed eyes at Paris gleaming through the casement windows. I look around for something heavy. I find a big ivory ashtray on the mantle. All things in moderation. If I hit him too hard and break it over his head, there's a good chance I'll kill him right off the bat.

"Julien?" I call out so he'll turn around and give me a profile. That way, I won't whack him at the base of his skull. For once, I get it just right. He pivots around, chin out, so all I have to do is tap his jaw with a quick flick of my wrist. The weight of the ashtray does the rest. He collapses on the cream-white carpet, the trickle of blood from his mouth barely ruining the perfection of the scene.

I pull my hand back for a second blow and lean over his body, but he's already out cold. This was not really my plan, but sometimes I lose my patience, especially with garbage like this guy.

I toss the ashtray aside and take a tour of the apartment. I go in the bedroom and turn on the lights. Nothing unusual, apart from the rubber dildo enthroned on the desk next to police handcuffs. I find his laptop and tap the touchpad, and the screen lights up. Just a few clicks and I realize the computer's brimming with the worst kinds of porn—garbage with kids and worse and I'm glad I lost my patience. I get a bitter taste in the back of my throat. Was this guy capable of killing Thibaut? My train of thought is short-lived. I hear a groan and turn around. Too late. Julien brings it down with all his strength right on top of my skull. The ashtray cuts right through my scalp. I can't tell if it's because I moved my head a tiny bit to the side, or because he was trying too hard and didn't aim right, but I don't pass out, even if it hurts like hell and blood's running down my eyes. We're on the ground, him on top, raining blows on me. I land one instinctively, right on his cheek—far from enough to lay out a guy as high as he is. I thrash around as best I can until a right connects with my chin. My guard drops, I take another hit, start blacking out, every blow that makes me see stars calling me back to my flesh, its resilience incredible when threatened with death.

"Hold up, hold up, please!" I beg. I can tell I have to. Fear always comes afterward, in hindsight, once the threat has passed and before the self-hatred born of shame sets in. That fear always played tricks on me when I was a kid, kept me from running with the predators. But right now, I just want to survive.

Wham. A brutal blow like a golf swing. Both hands clasped, hitting the corner of his mouth. I shut my eyes and wait for the emptiness. But instead, my attacker collapses next to me, and a pair of arms haul me to my feet.

"What the fuck is this? I got your message. You're lucky I was nearby." Cherif is furious. I'm just happy he's here, even if I'm still seeing stars.

"And who's this fuckhead?" he yells, pointing at Julien.

I struggle to catch my breath. I'm having trouble speaking. I sponge up the blood on my face with my sweatshirt. I want to reply, but it takes a few seconds before the words come out of my mouth. "It's...the guy who...raped Thibaut."

"What? Who's that?"

"The kid I'm supposed to find. This is probably tied to his disappearance."

Cherif rubs his face with one hand. He's about to lose his shit, but I'm too dazed to do anything about it right now. Julien's still out cold on the floor.

"Listen up, Idir. The cops are on my ass every day. They've got a thousand reasons to put me away. I live like a goddamn paranoid freak. And you, you jump a guy at his own place and ask me over. You think I need this? You think I don't have enough bullshit to deal with? No, you know what? Go ahead, just call the cops while you're at it. Tell them, 'You were looking for a chance to bust him, well here you go. He's holding someone hostage in his house.' I kicked the guy's door in because I heard you screaming inside."

"I think I'm going to barf."

"No, no—hold still and keep your eyes open. Now I'm going to tell you if this guy's guilty or not."

I watch him turn this way and that, a crazed look on his face, casting about for something. He sees the handcuffs and grabs them.

"What are you doing?" I ask, ready for the worst.

"You called me over here. So now you shut your face and let me do what I do." He grabs Julien's arm and drags his unmoving body over to the bed. Julien starts moaning. Cherif slaps a cuff around one foot of the bed and the other around his victim's wrist.

"The fuck are you doing?"

He makes no reply and starts slapping Julien lightly.

"The fucking hell are you doing?" I shout again.

"Shut your face," he says without looking at me. "Wake up. Wake up, shit-for-brains."

Julien mumbles, still groggy.

Cherif takes Julien's shoes off and starts in on his pants too. He really looks terrible in his boxers and his white shirt all covered in blood.

"Quit it, it's not worth it." I go over, determined to stop him, and grab him by the arm. He shoves me away and I find myself right back on the ground, nowhere near getting up again.

"You want to know if he did it? Well, let's ask him." He slaps Julien twice. "Where is he?"

No reply. Cherif gives him one swift kick below the belt. Julien howls in pain. "Where is he?"

Julien whimpers, "I don't know."

"Did you kill him?"

"Who the fuck are you talking about?"

Cherif kicks him again. "You fucking killed him, you son of a bitch!"

"I didn't do anything! Stop! Please!"

Cherif leans over Julien, pulls his boxers off and stuffs them in his mouth. I watch Julien on the ground, powerless, tears in his eyes, cock all shriveled up, purple from the beating.

"So that's how it is? Playing dumb? What did you do to him? You're a filthy pedophile, aren't you?"

Cherif pins Julien's legs, then takes a lighter from his pocket and starts moving the flame closer to Julien's crotch. He starts singeing hairs. Julien is choking on his own screams, mouth full of underwear. It's time I got up.

"Goddammit, stop," I mutter.

Cherif turns and looks at me in disbelief, like he's forgotten I'm there. He pulls the boxers from Julien's mouth and lets him speak.

"All I did was take him to the club! The rest was an accident. I never thought things would get so out of hand. I don't know what came over me. I was too high. I told him I was sorry." Tears are streaming from his eyes. His sobs are like the spasms of an epileptic midseizure.

"You were afraid he'd sue, so you killed him."

"No, no, I swear! I never saw him again after that!"

"If he'd killed him, he'd have confessed," Cherif says.

"Why'd you do it?" I ask Julien, who no longer looks anything like a torturer, just a terrified and harmless little douchebag.

"I knew he was a fag. Pretending all the time—I wanted him to know what he was, teach him a lesson."

I spit on him, a compact bloody gob. "And that's why you took him there?"

"It wasn't that bad. After all, it was what he liked."

I kick him right in the head. "How about that? You like that? Son of a bitch!"

I feel a pair of arms pull me back and my feet come off the ground. Cherif holds me there till I run of out oxygen. He lets me go. No way I'm catching my breath.

Cherif undoes the handcuffs and frees Julien. He grabs a

handful of Julien's hair. "We never came here, OK? You tell the cops, you press charges, I'll make your life a living hell. I know where you live. I'll find out where your parents live. Forget this ever happened, buddy."

Julien nods frantically, terrified.

"C'mon, let's get out of here." Cherif drags me out of the apartment. I feel like planes are taking off in my skull without permission from flight control.

The stairs don't make things better. If Cherif's arm hadn't been around my waist, I'd have sat down on the landing and stayed there bleeding on the doormat, waiting for it all to go away.

The street is deserted.

"I'm OK, you can let go." I regain my balance a bit. Wipe the blood off my forehead with my jacket sleeve. Fuck.

"C'mon, get in," he says, indicating a double-parked 4x4 with its hazards on.

I get in the passenger seat. The car starts. I know he's pissed off, and I'm better off keeping my mouth shut. But I need to know.

"Why'd you do that?"

"Why?" he shouts. "Because you didn't have the balls to! You should be fucking thanking me! You lucked out. I was having dinner with a chick nearby. If I hadn't shown up, who knows what he would've done to you! Did you see his eyes? Fucker was on vacation! Who knows how far he would've gone! Fuck me!"

He slaps the back of my head, sending a few more drops of blood onto the seat and the floor mat. He brakes violently.

"Get out of my ride. Get the fuck out!"

Slowly, I comply. The car tears off. I try to buck up. Where the fuck am I? I feel my skull. I really need to get sewn up.

I recognize the huge wrought-iron door, the surveillance camera above. With the migraine I have, it's a miracle I remember the security code. Luckily he lives on the second floor; I couldn't have made it up much farther. I knock. From inside, worried footfalls.

"Nadia, please, open up."

"Idir? It's three A.M."

"I know, I know...Can I come in?"

My father's significant other opens the door. She's wearing a white nightie and doesn't look very happy to see me. "Idir! You're bleeding!"

"Is Dad around?"

"Good God, what happened to you?"

"Oh nothing, I just fell. Can you get my dad, please?"

She opens the door and lets me in. One last look of dismay, and then she says, "All right. I'll get him."

Despite the pain, I catch myself checking out her ass as she heads down the hall. Soon my father shows up in his pajamas. He shakes his head at the sight of me. I smile, happy to see him. He doesn't look so happy though. On the living room sofa, he examines my scalp, his tiny glasses at the tip of his nose. "You'll need four sutures, maybe five."

"OK. I trust you. You're the doctor."

"I'll get my supplies. I'll be back." He returns with a needle, thread, scissors, rubbing alcohol, and a bowlful of water. He cuts my hair from around the wound and starts sewing me up. "You should've learned to do this. At least it's something I could've taught you that would've been of some use to you."

"I should've—"

"There are lots of things you should've done. Like not get mixed up in this kind of business."

"It's my job. It happens, is all."

"And what exactly is your job?"

"Dad, drop it."

"What do you want me to do? Feel sorry for you?"

"I don't want anything at all."

"Then why are you here?"

"To get stitched up."

"So you do want something."

"You're nicer than the internist at Lariboisière."

"Hold still, I'm almost done. All right." He ties a knot and snips the thread. He gets up; I stay seated.

"Thanks, Dad."

"You're welcome." He takes off his glasses and holds them in his hand. "You can go now."

"Everything else good?"

He smiles sadly. "Idir, in three hours I'm getting up to go to work. You don't have to pretend with me."

"What?"

"You know, Idir, I couldn't care less about your life. You're way past thirty and still running home to daddy when you get beat up. Fifteen years ago, it was the same story. Back then, I'd tell you not to get into fights. You were a child. But now you're a grown man. You can do whatever you want with your life. I'm not footing the bill anymore."

"Sorry I woke you up. Thanks for the stitches." I leave the large apartment and smash my fist in rage against the glass cage of the elevator.

CHAPTER 4

IN BED, EYES OPEN. THE PILLOW STUCK TO MY SKULL WITH
coagulated blood. My first headache of the week that isn't from
alcohol and a rotten mood.

In the bathroom, I shave my head, first with clippers, then
a razor to even out the cut and not have patches. My hair was
going already, so it's not that bad. I take care not to get too close
to my wound. Once I'm done, I reflect that it may not have been
the best idea. A bare skull striped by a purple-red gash—not
in very good taste. I foresee a week of getting stopped by the
cops and not getting laid. Not that my sex life is exactly thriv-
ing anyway, but with my gouged-up head, I'm absolutely sure I
won't touch a woman any time soon.

A shower rinses morning sweat and rancid odors from my body.

Once I'm dressed, I have a coffee in the living room. My gaze
falls on the tapes piled up on the table. Haven't the courage to
given them a listen. I'm not sure I'm on the right track anymore
anyway. I need help. I grab my phone. She picks up right away.

"Hey, Idir, how's it going?"

"Never better. You?"

"OK."

"I'm calling 'cause I need some help. I'm looking for a kid. He
left some taped confessions—might take a specialist to analyze.
I need an outside opinion, and since everyone I know is kind
of shady—"

She cuts me off. "You're asking me for help?"

"Think of it more like an invite to play amateur detective. Can you come over? I'm not going anywhere."

"I've got some things to do, but I'll drop by when I'm done, say early evening?"

"Thanks. See you then." I hang up. I knew she'd say yes.

Nat shows up around seven. When she rings up, I suddenly realize I'm nervous—just the idea of being alone with her in my little apartment.

"I didn't tell you everything on the phone," I admit. "The guy I'm looking for is Crumley's brother. I know there was...something going on with you two, so if you're not comfortable listening to this, it's completely understandable."

She looks at me like it's all the most normal thing in the world. "I'm fine with it."

"Good. To make it quick, the kid's twenty-two, gay, surrounded by assholes, and afraid to come out. He's very intelligent, clear-eyed about the crowd he runs with. I'm guessing he isn't like most people of his generation. He didn't record this to be heard; he did it for himself, hiding it on old Memorex. He rarely mentions names, places—I don't know much. Except that he was sexually assaulted in a nightclub by someone he knew. I found the guy, a first-rate son of a bitch, but he's got nothing to do with the disappearance. I think the kid ran away, alone or with someone, but I'm not sure of anything." She listens attentively. I finish up. "So I need your opinion, any kind of clue I might've skipped over, anything that could shed some light on where he is, who with—"

She cuts me off with a determined air. "OK, I'm ready."

Soon enough we're on the sofa, sharing my old pair of headphones like teenagers. A quick shiver right when I slip the tape into the Walkman, and I feel her breath, a whisper on my skin. The wheels start turning. I watch the gadget in my hands before hearing that now-familiar voice:

I'd done it before. My brother made me, to prove I was a man. He was the only one who hated me back then; now I hate him too. I was fifteen. He made me come to where the girl was waiting, served up on a platter. He told me to go to it. He was naked. I could sense a sort of unwholesome arousal at the sight of me doing it, the sight of me naked. They were both chuckling as I tried to finish as fast as I could. But I couldn't. I cried; their laughter became shouting. The girl pushed me out of her—my brother took over and told me to watch carefully. I ran away—they were still laughing. I still don't know why I wanted to do it again, just what I wanted to prove. It's proof I haven't managed to get rid of everything they put in my head. Every step forward counts. Next time, I'll forget everything and move on without thinking of them, just myself. Me, me, me. It's not the best solution, but I don't have a choice anymore. If I want to stop suffering...

I sneak a quick glance at Nathalie, who swallows discreetly.

... I'm not going to put up with this all my life. I'm going to get away from here. With him, if he wants to. He didn't interest me before. But he noticed how anxious I felt after I was assaulted. He didn't push it with me; he wasn't one of those people hooked on good works, who note down in their ledgers every hand they've ever reached out to someone. He was just there, ready

to talk when I wanted to, quiet the rest of the time. It counted for a lot in my recovery.

The tape goes on. She listened attentively. I watched her, obeying when she asked me to rewind, my fingers running over the Walkman's fat plastic buttons.

"What are you doing?"

I'd just pressed stop. "Aren't you hungry? I'll make us something to eat, help us see straighter."

She gets up from the sofa and stretches, still muzzy from listening.

"Want a beer?" I ask.

"I think I need one."

"Follow me."

She joins me in the kitchen. I hand over a can and start putting together a rudimentary meal.

"I didn't even know Oscar had a brother. He never mentioned him."

"He doesn't seem to have liked him much," I reply. I turn my back to her; it's probably easier to ask her questions that way. "Was Oscar already like that back then?"

No answer. I can tell I've made her uncomfortable. "I mean—"

"Idir, do you want to know if I was the girl in the tape, the one he forced his brother to fuck? No, it wasn't me."

"Sorry."

"No harm done. If you want to know, the only thing I remember from back then was dealing with a guy so high he usually had a hard time getting it up. As for his perverted side, I never saw it. He was an asshole, but so were lots of other guys. I'm not going to rewrite history now that I've heard that."

We eat in silence, wrapped up in our thoughts, still prisoners of ghostly reels of tape. When I clear the plates, I'm surprised to find her already on the sofa, earphones on, in a hurry to start listening again.

New cassette:

I went to see Dad at the hospital today—he's in a bad way. It pained me, seeing him like that; he was always so active, always explaining what it was to be a man, never understanding that you can't change the way you are and that people who give lessons and pointers are more ridiculous than anything. I still found him ridiculous, dead inside, in a dressing gown, a terrible smell coming off his skin. Decay. I felt sorry for him, the way you feel for a guy who got it wrong, spent his life prospecting for gold without finding a nugget. My mother cried. That didn't surprise me. She's vanished into her role. She saved me, made me with him, so I wouldn't want for anything. Despite everything, I respect that sacrifice. She finally kissed him. She forced herself for nothing. I'm not even sure he recognized us.

I stop the tape and look at Nat. "That's enough for tonight; I don't want to take up too much of your time. Thanks for the help. I've got a meeting with Oscar tomorrow."

She takes off the headphones, almost disappointed. "And what are you going to tell him?"

"What I think. That Thibaut ran away, and he'll be back."

She's looking off, her gaze lost in the distance.

"You're not convinced."

She replies hesitantly. "No, yes, I mean—I don't know. I'm tempted to say yes, but at the same time..." She stops for a moment, looks at me. "Can I borrow these? I'll give them another listen at home and give you an official opinion."

I don't remember her ever asking me for anything. Good thing too, because I wouldn't have said no a lot. She leaves with all the tapes, and I'm all alone again in my apartment.

The same café as last time. He's already there, looking anxiously around. He gets up to greet me, his eyes full of hope.

"Any news?" he asks before I have a chance to sit down.

"To be honest, no—nothing concrete."

"Then why'd you drag me here?" he retorts curtly.

"Look, I'm going to be honest with you. I think your brother ran away. He left to get away from it all for a while. But he'll be back. In a few weeks, a few months. But it won't be more than a year."

"How can you be sure?"

"You know your brother was gay?"

"I suspected. So what? It's his life."

That's right, asshole, pretend to be tolerant.

"Of course," I reply innocently, "but I don't think it was well regarded in his crowd. If you ask me, he left Paris so he could live freely. I don't know him, but I promise you your brother's worth more than that shit-heap he calls his social circle. I think he just needed a change of scene for a while." I decide not to tell him about the rape. It wouldn't do any good. "So there's no need to pay me. The expenses stop here. I won't find anything else. Just be patient, Thibaut will be back."

He remains pensive for a moment, then picks up again like our conversation never happened. "I'd like you to keep looking."

"I just told you, it won't do any good."

"I'll pay you more."

"I won't find anything else."

He looks at me, wild-eyed. I try to explain; I don't know why he's insisting, especially for someone he most likely despises in private.

"Look, I'm not the kind of guy who takes money for something when I'm sure I won't get any results."

"Fine, OK, I understand. I'll give you what I owe you." He pulls a wad of money out of his wallet. Small bills only—he actually made an effort. I count them again and pocket them.

"Thanks anyway," he says with apparent sincerity. "For everything."

"You're welcome. I'll call you if I happen to learn anything new." I get up.

"It'll be OK. He'll be back," I say, patting him on the shoulder.

I walk off, leaving him alone. I never thought someday I'd feel bad for that guy. The sight of him looking so lost momentarily weakens the hatred I've stewed in for years where he's concerned.

I go home and lie down on the couch. The meeting has exhausted me. I put a movie on. *Pickup on South Street*. Sam Fuller. Widmark's barely pilfered the wallet on the subway when I fall asleep. When I wake up, the end credits are rolling. I check my phone and see a message from another thief—a car thief this time—in my voice mail. Cherif asks me to call him back.

"Hello, Cherif?"

"Yeah."

"Look, about last time, I—"

"Yeah, yeah, fuck it. I—"

"No, seriously. I'm sorry."

"I said fuck it! You gonna let me talk now? Some guy spotted your car."

"Seriously?"

"Yeah."

"You the man!"

"Meet me in twenty near Saint-Blaise; we'll go together."

I find Cherif on his phone, leaning against his car.

"Well?"

"This guy in Bagnolet wants a chat with us. Got money?"

"Money?"

"For the guy."

"Uh, no?"

Cherif shakes his head. "You're a real dipshit."

After Cherif agrees to spot me the cash, we drive to the Bagnolet projects—two gray buildings a few stories high. Cherif makes a call. "Yeah, I'm down here. Yeah, the black Touareg."

Two minutes later, a young black guy, eighteen at the most, gets in the backseat.

"I'm listening," Cherif says, staring into the rearview.

"I want to see the money first."

Cherif snaps around and looks him in the eye. I turn around too. The kid's nervous, looks down at his shoes.

"Listen up, Mr. Big: you'll get your money, you have my word," Cherif says. "Now talk."

The kid hesitates before giving in. "This guy around here has the car. His name's Stephan."

"Is that all? Are you fucking kidding?"

"He's got an older brother named Claude. Claude Louasse. There was a shoot-out at a parking lot in Tremblay last week. Made the news. Seems Claude was involved. They said it was narcs, but that's bullshit. He's lying low; no one's seen him since."

"Why is it bullshit?"

"Those guys aren't drug runners. They're into more full-contact stuff—armed robbery."

"Go on."

"The day after the shoot-out, Stephan went around everywhere trying to unload the car. He was freaking out. He told everyone about it. He was ready to slash the price, he needed to sell; that much was obvious. Everyone could tell he was afraid too. And that was just weird. Nobody's ever seen him like that."

"You think he needed the money to stash his brother?"

The kid shrugged. "Not my call."

"Know where he lives?"

The kid nodded.

"Take us over?"

"That'll cost you."

Calmly, Cherif opens the glove compartment and takes out a snub-nosed pistol. He turns back to the kid and says, "This what you need? Is this what it's gonna take for you to stop thinking I'm your bitch?"

The kid starts to panic. "It's cool, man, we're all cool here. I'll take you."

"Well, there you go." Cherif puts the gun away and starts the car.

"Why are you giving up a guy from your own hood?" I ask.

"That son of a bitch would kidnap his own mother to get money from his dad. I got nothing to do with him."

"How old is this guy? What's he look like?"

"Twenty, twenty-five? I don't know. White brother from the projects."

That fits with the description Eric's driver gave.

He directs us to a street in a suburban residential area. "That's it—third one down."

Cherif keeps driving and pulls over into an intersecting street fifty yards down.

"Everyone out," announces Cherif.

"I'm staying right here. I don't want nothing to do with this," the kid says.

Cherif gives him a look; I signal him to drop it. He grabs the gun from the glove box and sticks it in his belt. The house has a small front yard of yellowing grass, its only residents a grill and an old plastic table, hemmed in by a rusty metal fence. Not exactly your upstanding Parisian's dream of a place in the country. Something tells me the owner isn't the type to do his own gardening, but really the whole thing just looks deserted.

"You sure you want to bring that?" I point at the hidden gun.

"Why, you think I'm going to show up at some psycho's house not packing?"

"You know, I'm a firm believer in the theory of conflict escalation."

He doesn't seem to be paying much attention to me. "What's your read on this guy?"

"No idea."

"You think he'll be nice and open the door?"

"Why not? After all, you have a gun."

"Idir, has it not occurred to you that he might have one too?"

As we get closer, I realize the gate in the fence is shut but not locked.

"I'll go around back," says Cherif. "This is your gig. I'm not about to take a bullet. Wait a minute before you knock."

He circles around back and lets me enter the yard alone. I grab a barbecue fork from the grill, hold it flat against my side, and head for the door. I sneak a peek at the weapon in my hand.

Pretty weak if the guy has a gun and is used to using it. I knock once. Then again. After thirty seconds, I hear footsteps inside. I ready the fork.

"Don't do anything stupid, it's me." Cherif opens the door.

"What the fuck are you doing?"

"The garage door out back was busted."

"Anyone around?"

"Yeah," he replies.

I follow him into the darkness.

"Don't you touch a thing," he says.

The house is a mess, but the air itself is worse—a terrible stench. A short hallway leads to the living room. The guy we're looking for is sitting on his sofa in front of the TV.

"Which one of them you think it is?" asks Cherif.

"No idea."

The man has a red hole in his left cheekbone and another in his heart. Apart from a homeless man I found frozen one particularly harsh December on rue des Couronnes when I was a kid, this is the first dead person I've ever seen. I have a hard time believing it. I wonder if I'd think it was as awful if it weren't for the smell. Cherif shakes me out of my trance.

"Whoever did this wasn't from the projects. It was a clean job. No Parisian gangbanger knows how to shoot like a goddamn sniper. What's the matter with you, anyway? What are you looking at? We have to get out of here."

"Just give me two minutes."

"That's it. I'll go wipe off the doorknob."

We split up. I make the rounds of the house. A small kitchen with dirty dishes. Nothing interesting. I find the bedroom in back. The bed's unmade, and the air smells of tobacco and mustiness. Lots of butts in an ashtray, porno magazines, a gun, and a GPS. I grab the GPS, stuff it in my jacket pocket, and head back down to the living room. Using a handkerchief, I go through the coffee table in front of the TV, watched over by the cadaver of one of the two brothers.

"The fuck are you doing?"

"I can't find the keys to the car."

"Drop it," Cherif says. "Whoever came by must've lifted the car too. Or, possibly, he had time to unload it somehow before he died."

"So where's the money?"

"Idir, fucking save the questions till we're gone!"

I take one last look at the dead man before leaving the premises.

Outside, I run around, looking for a luxury car parked among the residential streets.

"The fuck are you doing now?"

"I have to find that car."

"It's not here, goddammit! Get that through your head! C'mon, get in."

———————

Back in the Twentieth now, after dropping our snitch off in a shitty-looking OTB bar.

"Coffee?" Cherif asks me.

"No, whisky—and a beer."

He goes to order. I realize my hands are trembling. I think back to the dead man. Cherif comes back and sets the glasses down on the table. I down the whisky in a single gulp and start in on the cool beer right away.

"You were thirsty," Cherif says.

I feel my neck muscles relaxing and sink down into the seat a little more.

"What's the matter?"

"Why do you think he got killed?"

"No idea."

"Cherif, don't treat me like a moron."

"What do you want me to say? That guy wasn't going to die in bed of old age. All you have to do is find a car."

"Yeah, a car, not a fucking dead body. Besides, you said it. Whoever did that was no amateur."

Cherif starts laughing.

"What?"

"Idir, the guy who stole that car was a hard case, a psycho who kidnapped people for rent. If you don't want to see stuff like that or get shot or stabbed, stick to runaway teens and cheating wives."

I get up and dig in my pocket for change. Cherif waves me off to say he's got this round.

"If you hear about an R8 for sale, say I'm buying and put me in touch with the seller. Thanks for everything, ol' buddy."

———————

Back at my place, I have a big glass of water and lie down on the sofa. I turn up my jacket collar, wedge my head against the armrest, and close my eyes. I think the tears are about to come but all that comes is sleep.

The doorbell rings. Again and again. I open my eyes and, in no hurry, go to open the door, still groggy. And here comes a nasty blow to the head. *Nice to meet you too!* I fall over backward. The pain is spreading through my reopened scalp. My father's stitches won't be much good now.

The guy drags me by the collar into my living room. I open my eyes, awash in my own blood, and realize he'd hit me with the butt of his gun.

"The fuck were you doing at my brother's?"

A wave of inspiration helps me connect the dots. "Claude—" I manage.

Bad idea. I get hit again.

"How do you know my name?"

I'm too panicked to talk. He sticks the gun to my cheek and pushes hard. Warmth suddenly trickles down my thighs.

"Look at you, pissing yourself like a little bitch." He chortles. "The fuck were you doing at my brother's?"

"Stop, please. I was just looking for a stolen car, is all."

"Don't give me that bullshit! I was hiding right out front—I saw you come out! You and that other guy. Then I followed you here."

"He was dead when we got there. I don't know who did it."

He hesitates a few moments, then points at the sofa with his gun. "Sit."

I do as he says.

"I want to know who killed my brother."

"I don't know."

"Listen up," he says, "the only thing you can negotiate for is how long this is going to last."

I can feel something pressing against my back, behind the sofa cushion. "I swear I don't know who killed your brother."

He turns the barrel away from me. I know he's about to pistol-whip me again. I feel like I'm moving with incredible sluggishness. Like he'll have time to shoot me in the head, and my body will fall at his feet and then he'll dance on it. Still, I'm moving, and I manage to grab the Walkman and chuck it at him. It hits him right the face. Before he figures out what's going on, I slam into him full force below the belt. He goes down beneath me, and I hear his pelvis crack. I seal my fists shut with my thumbs, keeping them wrapped around the bones of my fingers, and start hammering his face and temples. I keep it up for a long time. Something has come loose. I do not stop. Not until his face is just shapeless mush, a blend of saliva, mucus, blood, and broken teeth.

Finally, I let myself fall to one side and throw up. A lot. I drag myself over to the bathroom, tear off all my dirty clothes, and take a shower. My fingers are twice their normal size, my knuckles split open just like the wound on my skull, which is gushing blood. I stay under the spray of warm water for a long time, like it's going to help make the body in my living room disappear. Without toweling off, I return, naked, to the living room to look at what I've done. Reality does me no favors. It wasn't a dream. He's still there. His gun, a huge piece that looks like a .45, is still lying in his open hand. I grab it and hide it in the kitchen drawer with the flatware. I know full well I've done something irreversible, something way above my head, something I won't be able to handle alone. At this point, I still may have a choice. But I prefer to believe the opposite.

They're all looking at me sideways. Naturally, Hakim's not around. Naturally, I don't recognize a single one of them, not even by sight. It's a brand-new team. Three sneaky-looking weasels: two goons and a little guy. They're all young, pushing twenty, just starting out, and they know the harder they are, the more they'll rake in.

"I'm here to see Tarik."

The little one, mismatched in tight jeans and a tracksuit jacket, comes over flashing a grin that's all teeth, no friendliness. "And just who are you?"

My skull's got a nasty gash in it, my hands are in tatters; I'm pretty sure I've never looked better. And my last nerve is shot.

"I'm a friend of his. Call him."

The little guy gives a nervous titter and turns toward his buddies. They're sizing me up. It doesn't look so bad. If they'd really wanted to lay me out, I'd already be crawling around looking for my teeth. But I'm in a hurry, which is the only thing that plays against me.

"Look at you—you look like a crackhead! You're spilling blood everywhere. Beat it before I get annoyed."

"If Tarik finds out I came by and you didn't tell him, he'll take you down a few notches."

The little guy draws his gun. I raise my voice. "But if he finds out you raised a hand against me, he'll cut your balls off. So one of you take out your cell phone, cross the street for a phone booth, or make some goddamn smoke signals, because I need to see him right now!"

I add, in a calmer voice, "Tell him it's Idir."

They all exchange another round of looks. One of them finally decides to get up and leave the bar. "If you lied to us, you're dead."

Tarik comes in a few minutes later. He can tell from my face I didn't drop by for some mint tea.

"Is it serious?"

"Yeah."

"What is it?"

"You'd better come see."

"Fuck me! You sure did a number on that guy."

I told him the whole story on the way over—well, almost. I didn't tell him about the other brother, the one I ran into first, dead on his own sofa. All I told him was about a guy hiding in my stairwell who jumped me and tried to rob me. I'm not sure he believes me, but I also don't think he gives a damn. Tarik doesn't need to know much more.

He takes his phone out and dials. I don't even know what he's saying, completely absorbed by the body on my rug and the blood that, bit by bit, is taking over my apartment floor as it dries. He hangs up.

"The kids'll take care of this for you. On me. But leave 'em a little something, because they're putting it on the line for nothing. Ten grand should cover it. OK? I called them; they're coming over. Once they're here, just do what they say."

"Thanks."

He slaps me on the shoulder and gives me a wink. "Hang in there, buddy."

And just like that, he's gone, like he's given up trying to start my car and called a tow truck instead. I hide out in my bedroom, unable to face waiting with the dead guy. I open up when they ring. The same bunch of shitheads who greeted me so warmly earlier, with the nervous little guy as their front man. They come in without saying hello, unimpressed by the spectacle and critical:

"Shit, man, you couldn't have done this cleaner? I mean, fuck!" The little one gives orders to the two others. "Go back the car up and bring in the tarps."

The two guys obey nonchalantly. I find myself alone with the little guy.

"Funny, you coming into the bar earlier, looking like some old junkie. But this is why you were all unhinged! You weren't kidding." He smiles and adds, almost like he gives a shit: "This'll give you a few sleepless nights."

The idea seems to amuse him. I wonder what kind of guy he is to be used to all this at his age. "How about you?"

He smiles again. "I might have some trouble sleeping. But just tonight."

The two men come back with several yards of opaque plastic sheeting.

"Pick him up and stick it underneath."

The two men do as they're told.

"Well, this is going to take a while, so—" He looks around at the blood on the floor, sighing. "Give me your keys."

"What?"

He says it again, enunciating every syllable, just so I know he doesn't enjoy repeating himself. "Give me the keys to your a-part-ment."

"No, I can't."

Another sigh. "Look, dude. You're fucked. You've got blood all over your face and hands; it's a miracle the cops didn't pick you up when you came by. There's a fucking dead body in the middle of your living room. Just look at the damn rug. If we don't do something, it's going to start raining blood on your downstairs neighbors. We're here to bail you out, bro. But it's going to take some time. We can't just walk down Pigalle with your body under one arm. Get it?"

"Uh-huh."

"I can see you're freaking out. But staying here while we do our thing isn't going to do you any good. Because your apartment is going to look like a Rungis-style slaughterhouse for a few hours. Tarik told you to trust me, right?"

"Yeah."

"Then trust me. Give me your fucking keys and take a long, long walk. I'll call you when it's over, OK? And when you come back, this'll all feel like a bad dream."

I take the keys from my pocket. Probably a dumb move. But fuck it, I have no choice.

"C'mon," he says, no doubt short of inducements. He takes the keys from my hand. I don't put up a fight. "You've made a wise decision, my friend. I'll call you when it's over, Scout's honor."

I leave the crew to do their work in my apartment and go out. Night is falling, and I decide to get some distance from my place in case anything goes south. I rent a room near Montparnasse. The hotel's empty. I pick the second floor so I can still jump from the window if the cops barge in. I try to take my mind off things so I leave the room and go to the movies. I pick a film at random and leave after ten minutes, unable to concentrate on anything but the consequences of what I've done. Go back to the hotel. The guy at the front desk gives me a sideways look. In the room, I block the door with the dresser. I lie down on the bed. I haven't eaten for a long time. Through the wall, I hear a couple fucking in the room next door. I've killed a man. I've known this feeling; I've had it before: the point of no return. A decision that changes the rest of your life forever. I picture a cell. The same one I slept in for six months. Except this one will be in supermax with guys doing hard time. I cry in silence, cry and cry, without letting out a single sob. The first time in years I've cried for an actual reason. And it goes on for a long time.

CHAPTER 5

THE WEE HOURS. A MESSAGE ON MY PHONE. I RECOGNIZE THE voice of the young guy Tarik sent over. He's saying I can come home now, the keys are under the doormat.

I go back to Pigalle. For half an hour, I circle my block without daring to go in. I can see plainclothes policemen on the café terraces—crazy paranoid. Finally, I punch in the entrance code. I push the door open slowly and go in. On the landing, my keys are indeed under the mat. I enter my apartment. Freeze for a few seconds in the dark. Turn the light on. Nothing. No more body, no more blood, no more smell. Like I'd dreamed the whole murder. I drop my coat on the couch. Still nothing. I search every corner, open the closets, look for evidence. Anything that might've been overlooked, that might prove my guilt. Nothing. They've cleaned house. The goddamned maids have been through. I'm happy as a kid who fucked up and by sheer force of will managed to wish it away.

Tarik's guy is in the bar, same place as last time. He sees me coming and grins. The two big guys aren't there; others have replaced them at the table. They're all sitting having coffee.

"Feels good to be home, right?"

Suddenly, I realize I owe my life to some dickweed barely old enough to shave with terrible fashion sense.

"Clean, right? We did a good job?"

A regular public works contractor. "Can I talk to you for a minute?"

He doesn't even need to send away the guys at the table. They've heard and get up all by themselves, packs of cigarettes in hand, overcome with a sudden jones for a smoke.

"Sit down. I'm all ears."

I take a chair. "I'll pay you what I owe you. I'm waiting for some money to come in. As soon as I get it, I'll give it to Tarik."

He shakes his head, as if to say I'm wrong. "You don't have to. We did it for the boss."

"I insist. You can split the cash with your friends."

"Count on it. Tarik was right. You're a stand-up guy."

I stick out my hand. "Till next time."

"If things get rough, you know where we are, right? We do quick, clean work."

I leave the bar, hoping with all my heart I'll never have to call on his services again.

I feel relieved. I don't ask myself any unnecessary questions. No guilt, just happy to be back at home, like nothing's happened. I open the windows; there's still a strong smell of detergent. I notice the rug is gone. Better that way—I'd rather not have some stranger's blood in my living room for good. I indulge in some spring cleaning of my own, scouring the apartment top to bottom. Two hours and a shower later, I lie down on the couch in my boxers with the last beer from my fridge.

The telephone vibrates: my father.

"How are you, Idir?"

"Fine, and you?"

"Fine. I'm calling to see if you wanted to have dinner with me at your grandmother's tonight."

"Uh—"

"It'll just be the two of us. If you have other plans, don't worry. I was just calling to ask."

"No, no, that's fine. I'm free tonight. Meet you over there?"

"I could drop by and pick you up, if you want."

"You won't mind?"

"I offered. Be out front at eight."

He's on time. So am I. I get in his Jaguar, a symbol of social success that's as much a reminder to our family as it is to the world. When I was born, he didn't have the means to treat himself to one.

"It's still weird seeing you driving this car."

"Why?"

"Dad, you're talking to your son here. Don't give me that. You're an Algerian, not an English lord."

He laughs. So do I. But it doesn't last long.

"What's with your head?"

"You'll never believe this, but I hit my head again stepping into the shower, opened it right up." I'm surprised there's no lecture, though he surely doesn't buy a word of what I've just said.

"I'll take a look at it later."

My grandmother opens the door for us. Squints right at my wound.

"What did you do to yourself?"

"Oh, nothing; just fell."

"I was talking about the haircut. You look like a convict. You're not a convict anymore, are you?"

I smile.

"So you decided to come back."

I keep smiling. "You upset?"

"No, never, not at all."

"Dad, was she upset?" I wink at him conspiratorially.

"She was very disappointed in your behavior last time."

She flies off the bat right away. "Nonsense! I just don't like drama, that's all. Well, if the two of you are done spouting gibberish, you're late, it's time for dinner."

I don't think I've ever known a stronger woman. She can't read, she's survived war and the hard life of a farmer; I always wonder if there's anything she couldn't endure. She never complains, except about other people. Her own she'd never say a thing about; she defends them like others defend human rights.

There's enough food for a family of twelve. Under my grandmother's watchful eye, I have to eat for at least two. My father is fairly relaxed. It's been a while since I've seen him this cheerful, especially in my presence.

"Did you see your son driving around in a car fit for a minister?" I ask my grandmother, just to get a rise out of her. "Soon he'll be demanding his couscous off a silver spoon."

"Don't speak ill of your father." She looks at her son, who's struggling to hold back his laughter, and launches into him next.

"You're no better. What do you need to drive around a flashy car like that for? Trying to get noticed?" she reprimands my father, who is now laughing out loud.

I start laughing too.

"And you stop making fun of him! That's it, this is the last time I'm having you over! The two of you are impossible! *Astaghfirullah!* You two are so complicated! Always up to something," she moans.

My cell phone vibrates, just once, in my jeans pocket. It's a text message from an unknown caller, whom I can tell has an international number, probably a Belgian chip. The message is in shitty French, but I understand it immediately. Cherif has found the car.

I get up from our cozy family table. "Work," I say in apology.

My father waves at my grandmother to leave it be. He really is on my side tonight. I kiss them both on the cheek and run out the door.

I reach Riquet out of breath. I wait a good five minutes, hand on my knees—next to ex-cons surely high out of their minds—before a car pulls up. The window goes down; Cherif's at the wheel.

"Well, what are you waiting for?" he says.

"You're always switching rides. How was I supposed to know?" I get in, and the car drives off. "So you sure this time? 'Cause all we found last time was a dead body."

I don't dare tell him about how Claude paid me a visit. About what I was forced to do.

"Your car's at Pareira's."

"Who?"

"One of the biggest resellers of stolen cars in the Paris region."

"So what are we waiting for?"

He gives me an apologetic look. "Better forget about it." "Why?"

"It's leaving for Morocco. Via Marseille. A guy over there bought it."

"Why not let my client buy it back?"

"Are you shitting me, Idir? Pareira'll know I ratted him out! Everyone who's anyone knows I was asking questions about your goddamn car. You're really riding my ass on this one, you know that? I'm a thief. I need guys like Pareira. He finds out I fucked him over, I'm dead."

"Oh, c'mon—"

"Look, Idir—that car? You're never going to see it again. End of story. Explain that to your client."

"I can't."

"What does that mean?"

"Find a way."

"Are you threatening me?"

"No. Not at all. I'm just asking you to find a way."

"I don't have one," he replies, furious.

"Well, I do," I retort.

"So what is it?"

"You know where this guy Pareira hides his cars?"

For a moment, he hesitates. "No."

Liar. I laugh: "I know you know everything about everyone you work with. You're fucking paranoid, I know you inside and out. You sure?"

"Fuck, Idir! Yes, yes, I know where he stashes them. What the fuck does it matter to you?"

"I'm going to steal it from him."

"What?"

"I'm going to steal it back."

He barks out a laugh, shaking his head. "You're nuts."

He looks me in the eye. "You realize if you try this, you're going to get killed."

"Look at you, always blowing things out of proportion."

———————

Cherif parks the car in the structure of a building on rue de Flandres. He has an apartment here, he says. It's pretty basic: a one-bedroom, comfortably furnished—in short, a nice place to lie low. I wonder how many of these he has. I slave away to make rent each month—maybe he could put me up if things get tough.

He takes two beers out of the fridge, opens them with his lighter, and hands me one. He vanishes for a moment, then comes back with a pen and a piece of paper. He lays the paper flat on the coffee table and draws a rectangle on it. With his pen, he points at his drawing and says, "Here's the warehouse. There's a gate with a guard at the entrance."

"And?"

"An alarm. Maybe a guy doing rounds, but I doubt it."

"That all?"

"That not enough? What do you think this is, *Mission: Impossible*?"

"Should be easy."

"You know how to take out an alarm?"

I look at him innocently. "No, but you—"

He gives me a dark look. "Me what?"

"Well, you do, right?"

He shakes his head. "No, Idir."

"What?"

"No, goddammit! I'm not coming with you!"

"Why not?"

He pinches the bridge of his nose, like he's got a migraine. "Idir, I'm not going to steal from a guy I work with. A business associate."

"Is he your friend?" I press the point. "Is he your friend or not?"

"No. He's a huge asshole. But he buys my cars."

"If he's not your friend, why the fuck do you care? He can never prove it was you." I add, "Besides, if he's an asshole like you say, it means you can't stand the guy. C'mon, it'll be like when we were kids again, for just one night, I shit you not. Like back in Belleville when we were just a couple of little fuckups, me on lookout and you—"

"Shut up!"

"We were ready to roll! We—"

"Shut the fuck up, Idir!"

I get up. "I get it, you're playing hard to get, that's cool. I'll go alone. But back in the day, you'd never have let a buddy down."

"You know something? I don't know why we're even friends anymore, you and me. What the hell have you ever brought me? Nothing but trouble."

———————

"You piece of shit," he hisses at me through his teeth.

I make like I didn't hear a thing.

Cherif is quiet, hands tight on the wheel. I knew he'd come. It was almost too easy. But far be it from me to complain. If he's with me, it's not just because he cares about me, but because he's into the idea too.

"Slow down, we'll get pulled over," I say.

He gives me a murderous glare.

"Kidding, kidding...just a joke."

He turns his focus back to the road.

"So—we there yet?"

"Open your mouth one more time and I swear I'll kick you out of the car."

We drive the rest of the way in silence. The warehouse is by Orly, a bit outside town, in an industrial area. Cherif parks the car by the sidewalk on an empty street, along a surrounding wall, and cuts the engine.

"The warehouse takes up the whole block. The entrance is over there, at the intersection. There's a gate and guards."

"So how do we get in?"

"Up there," he says, pointing a finger straight up.

"You mean we're scaling the wall? I thought you said nobody had to be Tom Cruise tonight."

"You got another plan?"

We get out of the car and close the doors quietly. He pops the trunk, takes out two pairs of stockings, two pairs of work gloves, and a whole bunch of stuff he crams into his coat before I can see what it is. He hands me a pair of gloves and a pair of stockings.

"Put these on. Once you're inside, do as I say."

I obey. The pantyhose smashes my huge nose flat, and I have trouble breathing. I feel like I'm eating a sock. "So how do we get up? You have a rope or something?"

"The roof of the car," he replies, annoyed.

He goes first. We must look like idiots, standing up there on the roof of the car in the middle of the night. Cherif is taller but lighter than I am. All it takes him is a quick jump to grab hold of the wall and hoist himself up. I try to follow suit, but my hands claw at thin air and I fall back noisily on the car. Ass perched atop the wall, like a fucking bonobo surveying his territory, Cherif shoots me an evil glare.

"You broke it, you bought it."

"Yeah, but I'll get a good resale price, with the roof the way it is." Second time's the charm.

The wall's fairly high. I know the landing will be rough, so I turn around, lower my legs down into the dark until the whole weight of my body is just hanging there by my hands, then I let go. I hit the ground hard, stumble, but my ankles hold. Cherif, who's landed without a hitch, helps me up.

"You are such a dumbass."

Before I have time to say that when you make a living as a thief, there are some things you're just better at—like breaking and entering—he says, "Not a sound from here on out."

The wall of the warehouse goes on several dozen yards. Heads down, bent over, we move through the night along this ocean liner of brick and sheet metal until we reach the corner by the entrance. Cherif freezes. He points at the guardhouse by the gate, where two men are sitting in front of a small TV. Luckily, there's a soccer match on. About twenty yards behind them, two sliding doors: the entrance all cars must pass through.

"There's a service door at the end. You stay here. I'll open it up. When I signal, join me. They can't see us. But they can hear us. So walk lightly, don't run like some fucktard," Cherif whispers in my ear.

He hugs the wall, going as slowly as he can, not making the slightest sound. I watch him, terrified, half convinced the two guys will see him. But they don't. Cherif makes it all the way over to the door unnoticed. He huddles over the lock for half a minute.

A quick click and he waves me over. I take a step and freeze. I'm scared shitless. Cherif waves his arm; he must be wondering what I'm doing. I'm suddenly trapped by the memory of Julien punching me on the floor. I think about death. About the barrel of Claude's gun. About my fear that this is it. About how I was starting to get a boner. About how I was saying my prayers, then chucked all that out the window when, lying in a puddle of my own urine, I'd begged him not to pull the trigger. What if those two guys over there heard me? No way. But what if one of them just stops watching his bullshit game for a second and comes out to have a smoke or stretch his legs? What if he sees me? Pulls his gun? Would I fall to my knees again?

I look at Cherif a few yards away, and my legs start working again. He holds the door open. I go through with him, and he shuts it without a sound.

"Goddamn," he whispers. "Don't move."

Blackness everywhere—I can't see a thing. I pull the nylon hose from my face and stick it in my jeans pocket.

Cherif pulls what I think is spray paint from his coat and starts shaking it, the metal ball rattling around the aerosol canister.

"What is that?"

"Polyurethane foam."

"What?"

"Shut up and stay here. I'll take care of the alarm."

Cherif starts walking along the wall. Soon I can't see him anymore. A few seconds later, I hear a *fshhh* pierce the silence. Then Cherif, speaking to me in a normal voice at last. "We're good. I cut it. Come on over."

Before I can remind him I can't see a thing, a flashlight beam shows me the way. I rejoin him by a long switchgear with the cover open. He's pulled the pantyhose off his face too.

"What about the cameras?"

"There are none," he replies.

"How do you know?"

"I deliver cars here. What kind of pro would I be if I didn't pick up on details like that?"

I suppress a smile, thinking that Cherif must have known he'd be breaking into this place someday. But he surely never imagined it'd be for me.

"Your Pareira's pretty stupid."

"He sells stolen cars. You think he really needs everything

that happens here on video? On HD for the prosecution?"

"So how do we find the car?"

He sticks the flashlight between his teeth while he digs around in his pocket and comes up with another one, which he gives me.

"Careful not to aim it too far. The plastic roofing's translucent; they can see the light from outside."

"Cherif, I don't know what it looks like."

"What? You didn't look?"

"I don't have Internet at home, remember?"

He sighs. "Stay with me. And don't touch a thing. Some cars might be alarmed."

That seems weird to me. If these cars are all stolen, their alarms should be neutralized. I wonder if Cherif is saying that because he's afraid I'll go around laying my hands on everything like some ten-year-old kid. Regardless, I keep my hands to myself and follow him past dozens of luxury cars parked in rows.

"There it is." He plays his flashlight across it. It looks more like a machine from the future than a car.

"You sure that's it? It looks like the Batmobile."

Cherif turns around. I can't quite make out his face in the dark, but it probably doesn't look friendly.

"What if there's another one?" I ask.

"Two R8s, stolen the same week? Anyway, we don't have time to go through them all. Your client wants that model, end of story."

Cherif walks around the car and then bends over the windshield. I figure Eric'll have to shell out for a new door, a new window, or both, but Cherif just grips the handle and opens the door.

"Unlocked?"

"Who'd come steal it?" he replies, getting in behind the wheel.

I climb into the passenger seat. With a stiff metal rod, Cherif forces something under the steering wheel. Then he takes a small electronic box from his coat and connects it to the bundle of cables now pulled out in the middle of the dash.

"What's that?"

"The thing that's going to let us start the engine."

I wonder how many magnificent toys are hiding in Cherif's black coat. He taps on the screen of his device.

"OK, so this is where things heat up. When I press this button, the engine is going to start. It'll take a few seconds, maybe a few minutes, you never know. What with the noise from the car, the guys outside are going to hear us."

"So?"

"So I need you to stand by the main doors. When you hear the engine turn over, open them up. I'll pick you up at the exit and we drive. Got it?"

"Yeah."

"But wait till you hear the car start, OK? And get that stocking back on your face."

I get out of the car and make my way over to the big doors, my eyes now used to the dark. The doors are fastened from the inside by a metal bar stuck through two rings of welded steel. I have to make a decision. Remove the metal bar now, or leave it? It might be heavier than it looks. One of the ends might hit the ground. Would the sound rouse the watchmen? Not to mention the door itself. I'm assuming they open easily, but the doors on my dad's garage have rusty hinges, and you have to push as hard as you can to slide them aside. Lots of questions. No decisions. Until I hear the engine turn over. A huge souped-up roar I didn't expect. It has to be the loudest car engine in the world. I yank out the steel bar, hear tires squealing. Door one is even heavier than I thought. I'll never get the other one open in time. And forget putting the stocking back on.

"It won't fit. I need to get the other door!"

"Get in! It'll fit!"

I dash into the car. Cherif hits the gas and we go through. It doesn't feel like it'll fit. Sparks fly from the body, the stucco wall and door saw the side mirrors clean off, but the car goes through. Outside, we find the two guys, dumbfounded. Cherif steps on the gas, heading straight for them. They dive at the ground to avoid us. The gate splinters, the car drifts left. Cherif spins the wheel, pulls gently on the handbrake, and straightens out the car, which misses a telephone pole by a few inches. My view of the road narrows; we're already pushing sixty. The rearview mirror—the one in the middle—is full of blinding headlights.

"They're already on us!"

"If we can make it to the ring road, we're good," Cherif says, yanking off his stocking and tossing it at me. He switches off the headlights and accelerates again; I feel a little like I'm in a spaceship floating in a dark galaxy—we can't see more than six feet ahead. Soon we end up on the highway encircling Paris. Then I understand why Cherif wanted so badly to reach open road. The powerful engine leaves our pursuers in the dust.

Cherif tosses a "told you so" my way with the grin of a partner in crime.

I wonder what we must look like, driving through Paris on a Saturday night at the wheel of a luxury automobile without side mirrors, the doors all scratched and dented. Thieves, surely—which is, after all, what we are.

"Well, what now?" he asks.

"I'll see if we can deliver the car tonight." I pull out my phone and dial the number Eric gave me for the guy who'd take care of the car. A man picks up.

"I have what you asked for."

"Where is it?" His voice is scrambled, like he's speaking through a throat-back.

"I'm in it, in the middle of Paris. Where do you want it?"

The guy gives me an address, doesn't bother repeating it, and hangs up.

I turn to Cherif, who's still focused on driving. "I didn't really catch much. He said he'll come for us by Porte d'Auteuil."

Cherif nods. We drive through the city, passersby and other drivers gaping at us, marveling at the luxury car and astonished by its laughable condition. Even if you live here, most people would struggle to drive through it without a map. Not Cherif. He knows every neighborhood, every crucial shortcut. It's a small miracle we don't run into cops on the major boulevards, where their presence is more less constant. Trocadéro, pushing farther west. The streets of the Sixteenth are empty, and I'm convinced the sound of the potent engine is waking people in their huge apartments, insulated as they are behind their double-glazed windows.

"We're nearing Porte d'Auteuil."

"Circle while I call again," I tell Cherif, pulling out my phone.

It barely rings. The same voice—now I hear a slight foreign accent in it, despite the scrambling—saying, "I see you. Pull in behind the BMW."

The line clicks dead.

"He said to pull in behind the Beemer. You see a Beemer?"

Cherif points right in front of me. There is indeed a car on the other side of the street, double-parked with its hazards on, just in front of the on-ramp to the ring road.

"OK, pull in behind him."

Cherif obeys, and we hug the BMW's rear bumper.

"So what now? Sit here with our thumbs up our asses till the cops come by?" asks Cherif.

I open the door, ready to get out. My cell rings.

"You alone?"

"No," I reply, just like that.

"You were told to come alone."

I'm getting tired of this little game of hide-and-seek. "I came with the guy who works with me. Without him, I wouldn't have the car at all. Now it seems to me that's what you came for. So are we just going to sit here or what?"

"Cut the engine."

"What?"

"Cut the engine."

I signal Cherif. The exhausting roar stops.

"Now leave the keys in the ignition and go home."

I hang up and look at Cherif. "He wants us to get out of the car."

"Why don't they get out? They're the ones who want the damn car."

"Don't make a scene."

We comply. The BMW's passenger door opens. A man in a bomber jacket emerges. What gets me, before I even notice his size or his height, is his face. He doesn't have one. Or rather, he has one, but it's hidden. He's wearing a ski mask. I'm not as well versed in the thugocracy as my childhood friends, but I know a few of its codes at least. And when a guy comes out wearing a ski mask in the middle of the night, that means something. Which seems totally out of whack with what he's come looking for. You wear a ski mask when you're picking up a shipment of coke, not to get a car when you're sure that car hasn't been followed. Cherif must feel the same way I do.

"Idir, what the fuck is this?"

Without a word, the guy comes over to us. He's probably counting on getting behind the wheel of the car and starting it up—I'm sure neither of us would lift a finger to stop him. At this point, the night can still end well. We even have time to go nurse a mojito, in peace, around République before going home to bed. But that's not counting the unmarked car—flashing light on the dash—that cruises right by us in slow motion. The cops who find themselves looking at two brown-skinned guys and a third guy in a ski mask, frozen in the middle of the street next to a luxury automobile with very dinged-up bodywork. They must be wondering if there's a camera hidden somewhere, or if we really are just a bunch of amateurs.

The rest goes by real fast. Turns out, Ski Mask is packing. He pulls an automatic weapon from his belt as quick as a trained soldier and opens fire on the cop car. Sparks fly from the hood. Cherif takes off; I follow. We cross the road at top speed. More shots from behind us, then the sound of engines. Two cars pass us by: the BMW and the car we brought them, leaving us alone, chased by cops. Running hard. I don't know the neighborhood. I don't know where we are. All I hear are sirens. Cherif ducks into a metro station. I think it's a bad idea, but I follow.

"Hide your face! The cameras!" he shouts as we hurtle down the stairs.

He pulls his hood up; I turn up my jacket collar. We hit the turnstiles like coming out of a slingshot. I haven't jumped a turnstile in years. My leg hits the bar; I take a blow to the knee. The sound of an arriving train. Stairs to the left, stairs to the right, fifty-fifty, but which? Cherif keeps me from having to choose by heading left. The beeping noise I've heard all my life. The doors close on a corner of my coat, but we're good. We're in. It's crowded, Saturday night and everyone looking at us—everyone always looks at the two assholes who make the subway at the last second. But the doors open again. Cherif risks a glance out the window. He sees cops coming down the stairs.

"The back. Quick."

We push people aside, clear a path. Two cops enter the car and try to spot us. A third waits on the platform, shouting at the driver not to leave. He's not wearing a uniform. The conductor probably thinks he's a nutjob. He gets scared when he sees the man running toward his cabin like a crazy person. So he restarts the train. The doors beep and the metro leaves, with Cherif, me, and two cops in the same car, radioing in for reinforcements at the next station.

"We get off at the next stop or we're dead," Cherif whispers.

I count the seconds in my head until the metro slows and the platform appears. I see Cherif's hand reaching for the door. I look at my shoes. The door opens. Cherif runs out first. I hear shouting behind us.

"Stop! Don't move!"

I tell myself they won't shoot me in the back. I speed up, not looking back, and hurl myself up the stairs behind Cherif. The street. I feel like we've gained a few yards on them. I also feel like my lungs are about to explode. Cherif points at a bunch of teenagers standing outside an apartment building. Music from the floor above. A party in a nice apartment.

"C'mon, c'mon, c'mon!"

He charges at the group, which drifts into the building without seeing us. The door closes. Cherif shoots forward, foot out, and kicks the latch from the lock. The door bangs against the wall, and I duck in behind him before it shuts again.

Cherif catches his breath, hands on his knees. Looks at me furiously. I lift my hand in a conciliatory gesture. "Sorry, man. There was no reason that should've gone down like that."

Cherif motions for me to shut up and presses his ear to the door.

"They there?"

"Can't tell. Can't hear a thing with the music." Back to the wall, he lets himself slide down to the ground. "Shit, we're stuck here. Fuck."

I go upstairs, following the music.

"The fuck are you doing?"

"Crashing the party."

"What?"

"What if a neighbor comes in and finds us here?"

The apartment isn't hard to find. The music's turned all the way up. We knock at the door several times. Cherif gives me a little slap on the cheek and grabs my chin, his red eyes looking into mine.

"If the cops come for disturbing the peace, and they—"

The door opens. A girl about twenty, too well fed to look comfortable in her little black dress, greets us, a glass of champagne in one hand.

"We're friends of—"

"C'mon in and have a drink," she says. No questions.

We follow her into the apartment. It's too dark for her to see the gash on my skull. The lighting probably makes my haircut look hip.

"What's your name?" she asks, glancing back over her shoulder.

"Uh—he's Jean and I'm Alain."

I turn to Cherif, who nods like a little boy. The girl bursts out laughing, spilling some of her champagne on the floor.

"Delighted. I'm Chloe."

We reach the end of the hallway. She waddles into a massive room with a parquet floor screeching from the torture of all those heels driving to the rhythm of violent electronica.

I try for a joke. "At least there are some hot chicks."

Cherif doesn't respond. He looks at me, jaw pumping like he's chewing some imaginary gum. Then he crosses the room, pushing people aside.

"Where are you going?" I shout in his ear over the music.

"To get a drink. I need one."

We go through several rooms, giant salons where the guests are spread out. They're all dressed to the nines: dancing, wandering down the hallways high, kissing—sometimes more—in the corners. The bar's a real bar, with a real bartender behind it. This is the first time I've ever seen anything like it. Goddamn, to think all these people are under twenty-five.

"What can I get you gentlemen?" the bartender asks.

I wonder if Cherif is going to burst out laughing or punch him in the fucking face. He goes for a third option. He orders. "I want a huge whisky. The size of a glass of Coke."

The bartender gives him a strange look. Takes out a glass. Starts to fill it. Cherif grabs him by the wrist and keeps him from righting the bottle till the glass is almost full.

"There. Nice job, buddy." He takes the glass. The bartender gives us another look and leaves the room. Cherif downs his whisky like it's water. It makes me want some, and I grab another bottle from the bar so I can drink straight from it.

"I have pulled some shit-ass jobs. But tonight was the shittiest of the shitty."

"I'm so sorry, man."

"Shut the fuck up and drink your whisky."

Soon the bartender comes back, another jerkoff in tow with the same model's face and frosted streaks. I wonder how any grown man can be that thin without appetite suppressants or serious bulimic tendencies.

"Who are you?" He doesn't look happy to see us. I try to explain what our grubby faces are doing at a party that seems as private as it does swanky.

"We're friends of—"

"Who invited you?"

"We came with, uh—Chloe. Yeah, Chloe."

"And who are you?" Cherif asks the guy, staring him down.

"The owner of this apartment," says the guy self-importantly. "And I don't know any Chloe."

Cherif suddenly starts beaming. "Aw, c'mon, sure you do."

He tugs at the guy's sleeve. The guy pulls his arm back.

"C'mon, man, she's over there. She's the one who brought us."

Cherif walks toward another room in the apartment, looking for the girl from before.

The other guy follows him. "No, not that way!"

Too late. Cherif has just walked into a massive bedroom.

"Ah shit, I thought she was over here."

Now all three of us are alone. The master of the house seems to be getting pissed off. "Gentlemen, finish your drinks and get out, or I'm calling the cops."

Naively, he thinks he's won the round. He turns his back on us to return to the other room. Big mistake. I see Cherif's hand hurtling toward the back of the guy's neck and, with a simple shove, Cherif sends his face crashing into the jamb of the door he was about to go through. The guy collapses, out cold.

"He was starting to get to me. Give me a hand over here."

Quickly, Cherif shuts the door and grabs the party's host by one foot, dragging him across the parquet. I take the other.

"Let's stick him under the bed, so he can take a nice nap and no one sees him."

We stash him under a canopy bed.

"You really KO'd him there."

"Shut your face. It's your fault we're here."

"So what now?"

"Now we wait for the metros to start running again in the morning and get out of here."

Sprawled on a dark sofa and with an eye on the closed bedroom door, we pass the bottle of whisky from the bar back and forth. Right in front of all those partying people. Music turned up to the max. Not speaking a word to each other. It's the ideal time to wonder why I'm such a fuckup. Why everything I touch always turns into a goddamned can of worms. I'm starting to feel drunk, which doesn't help things and makes me chatty.

"I found Claude."

"What?"

The music covers my voice. "I found Claude. Unless I mean Stephan—anyway, the brother of the dead guy we found. Well actually, he found me."

"What are you talking about? Stop drinking for a second."

"He jumped me at home the night we came back from Bagnolet. Stuck his gun right in my mouth. I pissed my pants. I begged." I swallow. A tear comes rolling down my cheek before I even feel it coming. "I killed him."

"What?"

"I killed that fucking son of a bitch. I paid a crew that rolls with Tarik to clean it up."

Cherif takes my head in his hands. "Hush."

"I fucking killed him! I—I didn't mean it. It's not what I meant to happen."

Cherif is whispering in my ear. I don't even understand what he's saying anymore; they're just words you use to comfort a scared child, waking from a nightmare.

———————————

Around six A.M., we leave the apartment with the last of the partygoers. From what I understand, most of them are planning to keep the night going at a private club in Wagram. We share a taxi with a guy who lives near the Opéra. Once we get there, we walk a little and then sit down at a café, savoring a coffee and a croissant in silence, squinting, blinded by the pallid day.

"That's some serious shit that happened to you," says Cherif in a tired voice, not exactly inviting conversation. He takes a sip of his coffee.

"I think I was naive. The guy who hired me was on the level, so—"

"What, a guy with his own commando unit that shoots at cops? You think?"

"All he asked me to do was find his car."

"Yeah, sure. And while tracking down the car, we find a dead guy whose brother tries to kill you in your own home and a goddamn giant in a ski mask shooting off his gun like it's Bastille Day."

"You don't understand. This guy, he talks to me just like you would, playing it straight."

"Maybe. But right now he's fucking you over like I never would. Keep that in a corner of your mind the next time you see him."

CHAPTER 6

AFTER A FEW HOURS OF SHITTY SLEEP RIPPED FROM THE DAY'S clutches, I decide to head straight over to Eric's office without trying to reach him first. I feel like I'm walking in slow motion through a massive movie set, in the middle of people scurrying everywhere. Still exhausted from the night before, I struggle not to fall asleep on the subway seat. Nearly miss my station, but I manage to get off at Champs-Élysées. The Champs. A few minutes later, I'm standing in front of Eric's secretary—the kind of girl who doesn't even look pretty anymore, despite a more than flattering figure. Just seeing how she draws her lips back in a sneer when I talk to her—she'd spit in my mouth if I asked her for water. I tell her I'm here to see Eric Vernay. Without taking her eyes from her computer screen, she says he's in a meeting. I tell her I don't give a shit. She picks up her phone and passes on the message. Then, with a limp finger, she points at the gleaming sofa across from her, which looks like it was just bought last night.

I barely have time to sit down before Eric comes hurtling out of his office. "Hello, Idir."

Composed as ever, that way he has of making you feel like everything's going great. *We're just good people here, working on your everyday problems.*

"Nice work. You here for your money?" He must see from my face that I probably want a bit more. "Is there a problem?"

"I want to talk to you for a minute."

He gestures for me to follow him and opens the door to a meeting room.

"You've got five minutes," he says, not bothering to sit down.

"Who took the car?"

He smiles. "I don't think that's any of your business."

"I think it is."

"It doesn't fall within your purview."

"Neither does getting caught in a firefight with the police!"

"That was unanticipated. Hazards of the trade."

"No, no," I correct him. "Unanticipated hazard is running into a carful of cops. Unanticipated hazard is a chase through the streets. Getting arrested. Doing time if you're not lucky and if it comes to it. But you never, ever open fire on the cops. Especially not over a fucking car!"

Eric keeps his cool. "I'll make sure you're well paid."

"That's not the point."

"So what is the point? You think you can march in here and lecture me? I don't pick people for jobs like this based on their résumés. So if I'm responsible for my guys, it's only up to a certain point. But I back them up all the way."

I shut my mouth, stunned by his words.

"I've readied your payment. Cash. I'll overlook the repairs needed on the vehicle."

We walk outside the meeting room. He signals to his secretary, who turns around and opens a closet. She takes out a huge leather bag and sets it on her desk. Eric claps me on the shoulder.

"There. Your money's inside. A pleasure working with you. Keep the bag, it's a gift."

"That's all he said?" Cherif asks.

I'm telling him about my meeting with Eric over mint tea at a café in Ménilmontant. "Yup."

"And you don't think that's weird?"

I shrug.

"Either you're really fucked up or you're hiding something from me. Whatever, I don't care." He gets up, looking tired.

"Cherif, wait—" I extend my hand. "Thank you, for everything."

"You're welcome."

"I'd like us to split the money."

"What?"

"You heard me. I want us to split it."

"Keep it, Idir. I make a living just fine."

"You never know. At least set it aside to pay some big shot if things ever go sour."

"OK, fine. Nice of you. Just don't jinx me, OK? The only thing I need to do to avoid things getting sour is stop hanging around with you. That's hairier than jacking a Ferrari from the Trocadéro on a Saturday afternoon."

"I'll write you a check."

"Idir, look at me. Do I look like the kind of guy who takes checks?"

I grin and hand him the bag with half the money in cash. "Kidding. Here. I threw in some for the kid in Bagnolet too."

He looks inside the bag.

"Count it if you want."

"No."

"Hey, Cherif?"

"What?"

"What a fucking night, right?"

"Go fuck yourself!"

"Save that for next week, your birthday maybe."

He gives me a smile equal parts sly and surprised. "So you didn't forget! I rented out a bar, but since I thought you forgot, I didn't invite you."

"You're such a bastard."

He laughs. "See ya. Ciao."

I watch him go. I know the whole outing turned him on. Goddamn sicko. I wrap up my Mr. Big Shot tour and give the rest of the money to Tarik. He promises he'll pass it on to the kids who took care of the body. I've spent all of Eric's money. There's nothing left.

My phone rings as I'm going upstairs to my apartment. It's Nat. She says she's in the area and asks if she can drop off the tapes. I tell her to swing by. Five minutes later, the doorbell rings.

"Oh, you...got a haircut. Looks nice."

I can tell she doesn't mean a word of it. "Thanks. Please—come in."

I close the door behind her. I can see from the rings under her eyes she's been crying, but I make no comment. "Sit down, sit down. Can I get you something to drink?"

"Yes, I'd like that."

I head for the kitchen and realize she's sitting in my living room. I wonder if she can smell death still lurking in the corners. If she comes across a scrap of brain I overlooked, what will she think? That I had dinner in front of my TV and didn't do a good job picking up after myself? She takes the tapes from her purse and sets them on the table.

"Here you go—that's all of them. I gave them a good listen, and—"

I cut her off. "Hey, uh, Nat—you eat yet?"

"No."

"How about a meal out?" I can see she's hesitating. "We'll discuss it over dinner. C'mon, you'd be doing me a favor. You're never in this part of town."

Next thing you know, we're both standing in the street. "I know a nice place a little farther up."

We walk all the way to Montmartre. The streets are crowded. She seems to enjoy the bustle.

"It's a change from your neighborhood, huh? There's more action out here in one night than in a year up by you."

She smiles and glances at me. "Don't make fun. I lived around here in my student days."

"Oh really?"

"Down that way, toward Poissonnière."

I didn't remember that. Maybe I'd never known. "No kidding!"

She smiles again. "Sure. I grew up in Essonne. I came here to study for college. My parents didn't have enough money to rent me an apartment, so I found a tiny garret. It was horrible, but I was happy. Not having to take the train into Paris anymore, are you kidding?"

Now I know why I'd never known, because back in the day she'd lied about it. She pretended, hiding the name of the godforsaken hole where she was from. She probably lost her virginity to some tracksuited creep who sold nine-bars at the local train station. Who might've done some time along the way. Who definitely had a shitty life today. And here I'd always thought of her as unapproachably upper crust.

"You hid it well. I was convinced you were the daughter of a cabinet minister."

She lifts a hand like she's about to hit me. "Stop teasing me!"

I don't take her all the way up the Butte—too easy. That's where some Parisian undergrad would take a Dutch exchange student. Instead, we stop halfway up at a Nepalese place. I find it weird, thinking like this, when she's been my friend for years. And my best friend's wife.

The restaurant is deserted. She picks a little table at the back. Once we've ordered and they've poured the wine, I bring up the case. "I'm sure the kid ran away. Nothing serious. He'll be back."

"I'm not so sure," she replies.

"How's that?"

"He's quite lucid about his situation. He's not just some spoiled kid doing some soul-searching. He knows what he is, what he wants—and what he's worth. He wants a long-term solution and these tapes play a part in that. Just running away for a while would be childish. And he's too brave to run away..." She stops talking. A few moments of silence.

"What's going on, Nat?"

She sighs. "Oh, nothing."

"Stop it. You didn't look well when you showed up. What's wrong?"

"It's Thomas. It's always Thomas. And if you ask him, it's me."

I smile. She gives me a murderous look.

"Sorry, it's just—isn't that how it's always been?" I say. "Ever since the three of us have known each other. It's been more than ten years. I think that's just how it works."

"I'm not sure I follow."

"Of everyone in our class, you guys were made for each other—king and queen, if you will. And you know what? I think even without your affair with Oscar, he'd have been pathologically jealous. You knew it before you married him."

"I hate him."

"Oh, come on—"

"Idir, you have no idea—"

"You're just saying that because things are complicated right now, because he thinks—"

"He's a piece of shit!" she shouts, then looks around. But the restaurant's still empty, and the waiters don't speak French that well. She tucks her brown hair behind her ears, embarrassed.

"You—you want to leave?" I ask, no longer sure I know what this conversation is about.

She frowns at me. "Leave? The restaurant?"

"No, leave Thomas."

"Maybe," she says, sounding like she doesn't really believe herself.

"Forgive me, but I'm not sure I understand. You're going through a rough patch, sure. I want to hear whatever you have to say. But if you want me to badmouth Thomas along with you, I won't go there. I'm not judging you. Just like I'm not judging him. After all, he's still my friend."

"Why does he mean so much to you? Without him, you could've stayed in school—"

"Stop—"

"You'd never have gone to jail—"

"Stop! Thomas never forced me into anything. All he did was make me an offer. If I was dumb enough to take him up on it, that's on me. It's on me if I wanted to prove I was a tough guy so all the world could see. And pretty soon, I figured out how stupid I was. Once I was in jail."

The waiter interrupts us with our entrées. Which is fine by me, because I hate dredging up memories from back then. I take the occasion to knock back my wine in one gulp and pour myself another glass. Nathalie sticks her fork into her plate like nothing's the matter and starts eating. "Delicious!"

"Glad you like it."

"Thanks for bringing me here. I really needed a night out."

"My pleasure. We don't see each other often...enough."

"What do you think Thomas would say if he saw us here together?"

"Nothing," I say, before digging into my dish.

"Nothing?"

"Nothing at all. He trusts me completely."

"But not me, is that it?"

I shrug and keep eating. We end up bursting into laughter.

"I think that of everyone in our class, you're the only one who never tried to hit on me. Why was that? I remember I was starting to get offended."

"What's with these questions?"

She laughs it off, but then insists. "Why? C'mon, give me an answer."

"You weren't my type."

"Liar! You were checking me out like everyone else!"

We laugh again. Then the laughter fades away and she's back to being stubborn. "Why?"

"I don't know. You were going out with my best friend. I—"

"Don't give me that bullshit," she says, leaning across the table and bringing her face close to mine, like she's going to kiss me. She's too smart and too sure of her looks to fall for baloney.

"I knew I'd never get you. Call it my pride. I'd never have let anyone touch it. Especially not you."

My response doesn't seem to surprise her, like she expects as much. "So my first question leads me to a second."

"Go ahead."

"Idir, when you beat Oscar to a pulp, why did you do it?"

"Sorry, I don't see the connection."

Her stare doesn't falter, and I realize I have to give her an answer. "I told you—to prove I was a badass, to be accepted, and for the money too."

"Nothing to do with me?"

"No, nothing."

"You swear?"

I look her in the eye. "I swear."

She knows I've just lied to her.

I insist on paying the bill. We head back out to the street. Cold has settled over Paris; the summer didn't last. She shivers. I notice and say, "We'll try to find a taxi fast."

"You heading home? Sick of me already?"

"No, I—"

"I could use a beer," she interrupts, looking around.

We walk to a bar nearby. The tables are overwhelmed by hipsters. We squeeze into a spot at the bar and order two beers.

"It's packed," Nathalie observes.

"It always is here. Get out of your tower a little more often, come and slum it up with us."

We laugh, banter a bit with the guys waiting at the bar, waving for the bartender to come over and take their orders. Prettier by a long shot than all the boho girls crowding the joint, it still takes Nat a while to get the bartender's attention. I smile, shrug to show there's nothing I can do. That's how Paris is. The bartender's a rock star; fully aware of the power he wields, he'll get around to you when he feels like it.

We finally end up with beer in our glasses again and I'm conscious—in this very moment—that this evening drinking pints with Nat in a bar full of students is quickly becoming the best night I've had all year. Without a doubt. Which either means I enjoy the simpler things in life, or that my life lately has been pure shit. But I pretend not to know which and leave the question hanging.

"Idir, you falling asleep?"

"No, no—just thinking."

"About what?"

"Oh, I don't know—our lives, the paths we've taken since we finished school. Well, I mean, it was a little different for me. My course got a bit...altered."

"I don't think so," she says, sure of herself, like she's worked me out a long time ago. She goes on: "I knew you wouldn't finish school because school wasn't for you. It was obvious you were looking for something, that you were uncomfortable, not in your element around us. But I never knew what was wrong. What you really wanted out of life. What you would've wanted to do."

I sip my beer and listen. What began as a simple swig turns into a glass-draining guzzle that gives me away before I confess, "I like doing nothing. I did look around. But that's the truth. I don't want a boss. I don't want to be my own boss. I'm not brave. I have no talents. I don't want a kid. That's it—all there is to it. After a while, it's pretty simple. If you haven't found the answer, it's because there isn't one."

"Too bad."

"Why? It's only too bad if you had plans. But I didn't. I always knew I'd never be a movie star."

"It's sad, I mean."

"No. You want me to tell you what's sad? Sad is when you believed in things, when you backed a man who turned out to be the wrong horse, when you wanted a career and wound up with a guy who makes a living taking out other people's trash, getting philosophical over a beer on a weekday night. Sad is telling yourself you made the wrong choice every step of the way and you're going to pay for it the rest of your life."

Tears well up in her eyes. She tries to smile the bad feelings away. She must know she can't. And so, without a word, she gets up and walks away, fast. I let her go, take one last long sip of beer. Long enough to realize how stupid I was and run off after her.

Outside, I scan the crowd of passersby all around and spot her in the distance. She's just crossed boulevard de Clichy. Cutting through the traffic, I almost get run over by a bus, but manage to reach her. She's paused on the sidewalk, looking for something in her purse.

"I'm sorry, I don't know what came over me."

"It's nothing, Idir. You're right."

"No, I swear, I don't know what came over me. I felt bad and I was looking for someone to hurt. Before that, it was a nice night. I don't want to ruin it."

"Too late. Thanks for dinner." She starts walking again. I follow her.

"You won't find a taxi right now. At least come by for a drink. Just one?"

We head back to my place. The beer that started off the evening was in fact the last, and there's nothing left to drink, just the dregs of a bottle of whisky that must've been hanging around for months. Still, I manage to pour us two decent-looking glasses.

I carry them to the living room, set them down on the coffee table, and sit on the sofa next to her. "Thanks for coming back."

She gives me a vague smile. I can sense something's broken in her. I reach out for my glass. She stops me, takes my forearm, and pulls my hand to her, to her chin, then the hollow of her throat, and then down onto one of her breasts. My fingers tense. She whimpers. I didn't mean to hurt her; I thought I was caressing her. I pull my hand back, ashamed. She comes toward me and kisses me. The rest doesn't look like much, just two bodies mingling to keep the cold night air at bay and the feeling of having missed out on so much.

Only on waking the next morning and looking at her naked in my bed do I notice the bruise on her breast. She draws the sheet up in an act of modesty that surprises me given our romp the night before.

"Coffee?"

She gives me a shy nod.

I return from the kitchen with a cup and bring it to her; she's still in bed. She blows on it and smiles. Is she used to mornings like this? A married woman waking in a lover's bed. I wonder how many coffees just like mine she's sipped to look as natural as she does right now, to succeed in making me believe everything's normal, that sleeping with your friend's wife isn't that bad, that after all, life is complicated enough already without adding another layer to it.

"I'm going to take a shower," I tell her, leaving her alone, blowing on her coffee.

When I come out, a towel around my waist, I can feel the apartment is emptier. She's gone.

The next day, I call her in the early afternoon. She doesn't answer. I leave a stupid message, a mixture of "ums" and "uhs" between apologies for calling her, apologies for bothering her, dozens of apologies, all for a single, fearful "call me if you get a chance."

I don't think anything will come of it, but she calls me just half an hour later. I ask her out for a drink. She says yes. We meet in a crowded bar by the Canal Saint-Martin. She's early. When I get there, I see her waiting for me outside, getting ogled by guys out for a smoke, glasses in hand.

"Is this OK?" I ask.

I don't lean in to kiss her cheek. Neither does she. She seems embarrassed.

"Shall we go in?"

She nods, and I find myself holding the door for her, then clearing a path for us to the only open table in the room.

"You OK? You don't look so great," I say as she takes off her coat.

She doesn't answer.

"You know, if you're not comfortable, we don't have to—"

She cuts me off. "Can I sleep at your place tonight?"

No question could've made me a happier man.

We stay naked, kissing in the shadows for a long time. My hand is on one of her breasts when the first sob hits me, making me seize up. Like a hiccup you try to stifle, so as not to draw attention. I start sniffling. No go; the first tears are running down my cheeks. She hears me sigh heavily, feels my face in the dark.

"Is it OK?" she whispers.

This is such bullshit, I think. "No, no, it's great," I breathe out in an asthmatic voice.

She's getting worried. "Is it me?"

"No."

"Thomas? Do you feel guilty?"

"No."

"Are you afraid?"

"No."

"Then what is it?"

I can talk again. The tears are passing, almost over now. "It's nothing. There's no reason for it. I—I've always had this. It's—it's like a condition. I know I look like an idiot, crying like a little kid, but that's how it's always been."

"Thomas never knew?"

I shake my head. "I hid it as much as I could."

She gives me a long kiss, her hand behind my head. I dry my tears on her face. She pulls me inside her. I don't know what happens after that. No sensation, no memory of anything. Not of coming, nor of falling asleep.

I spend the week with Nat. She shares my bed every night. Cravenly, I ask her if her husband suspects; she makes it clear that everything is under control and that it isn't any of my business. She leaves in the morning, and I stay and sleep. When I get up, not that unhappy to be alone again, I finish the coffee she's made.

Soon it's the weekend and Cherif's birthday. When I had asked him if I could bring someone to the party, he said no. So I decided to take Nat, because how could he say no to her? As for Nat, I struggled with how to bring it up to her: "My best friend's having a party tonight. You'll probably be the only girl there—well, what I mean is there'll be a few other girls: hookers, or girls who can lay me out with one punch, the line between the two being thin, maybe they're really the same kind of woman. Most of the guests will be men: felons of every stripe; best-case scenario, ex-cons out of the life or still practicing. I think that about sums it up—wait, no, one last thing: if anyone offers you anything to swallow, snort, smoke, or even drink, say no politely. And if you really want to say yes, out of actual desire or just fear of offense, come and ask me first; I'll tell you what you're getting into. Or warn me, at least, so I know why you're high all of a sudden. That's it! If someone tries clumsily to hit on you, you handle it. I can in no way get in a fight with anyone at this party. I like my teeth the way they are. Any questions?"

On second thought, I decide not to say anything and just tell her it's an old friend's birthday, that I have to go, and we can leave whenever she wants.

If Cherif has rented a bar out for the night, it's because he's totally paranoid and never has anyone over to his place, not even me—I only ever see him outside, at the apartments of his "associates" or in one of the safe houses he rents, sublets, or owns, I never know. I don't even know where he actually lives.

We show up late. I try to make my way through the delinquents, who seem pumped full of alcohol already. Nat follows me. Everyone stares. A peroxide blonde is already prancing around in a bra and lacy boy shorts, spilling a little more champagne onto the floor each time she laughs. I find Cherif alone behind the bar, pouring himself a drink. He smiles when he sees me. He smiles even more when he sees Nat beside me. He's plastered. He takes me in his arms, kisses me as I murmur, "Happy birthday."

He loosens his embrace.

"Cherif, may I present Nat."

"Happy birthday," Nat says with a smile that would make any man happy.

"Thanks. Nice of you to drop by."

I pull the wrapped gift from my coat and hand it to him.

"Oh, you shouldn't have."

He seems genuinely moved. The alcohol's probably helping, but still.

"Cut the crap, it's your birthday."

"What is it?"

"A book."

He makes a face. I see the vodka has killed his sense of humor but not his manners. "Oh, thanks."

"Kidding, Cherif! I know you can't read worth shit. It's a DVD."

He lets fly a crooked grin and tears the package open.

"*The Wild Bunch!*" He lifts the box in the air triumphantly as Nat looks on, astonished.

"I hesitated between that and another joyride around Paris," I joke.

Cherif leans forward, telling Nat like an innocent little kid I hardly remember ever seeing, "The one time this guy wanted me to skip school with him was for the movies. Back then, we thought he was a nerd, so I didn't want to go. But he said he'd buy my ticket, that it was a classic, so I went. Wham! Never regretted it. One of the greatest films of all time."

He turns to me. It looks like there are tears in his eyes. "This makes me so happy. We'll watch it together at your place next week. You come too, Nat. I'm counting on you!"

"It'll be my pleasure," she says.

He sets his gift on the bar, watches us with kid eyes. "Well, we boozing it up? What can I get you?"

A good dozen drinks later, after seeing all my old friends—and all the morons from my neighborhood—I stumble on Cherif talking with a lot of sweeping gestures to Nat, who's utterly at ease. I walk over, intrigued.

"I was telling her about our school days."

"Not like you stayed there long."

"See," he says, pointing at me, "I don't know what your relationship is, or how long you've known each other, or—"

His speech gets thick. If I hadn't drank just as much, and if Nat weren't a married woman but officially my significant other, I think I'd be afraid of what he was about to say.

"—but I've known this kid for a long time. I could go on for hours."

"Cherif, how about you stop? C'mon and dance, let me pour you a drink or something, but don't drag all that old stuff up again. She's a classy lady; she couldn't give a fuck."

"No, not at all," Nat retorts. "I'm riveted."

Cherif's too far past embarrassment not to go on. I know he's going to tell a story that makes me uncomfortable—I'm just not sure yet which one.

"We were hanging out on the stoop, we must've been thirteen, fourteen? Being little shits, we were bored. Our parents didn't like seeing us loiter around. But they had other things on their mind. Idir's father, though, would always come looking for his son. On his way back from work, he'd drag him away by the ear, humiliating Idir each time. We'd all tease him for it. Still, he took it. Despite that thick little skull of his, he had one thing straight. Even talking trash in front of his friends, he never disrespected his father. Never. The rest of us were already past saving; I think I'd have smacked my dad a good one if he'd shown me up in front of the assholes I hung out with back then. But Idir, he knew who his father was and what he owed him."

"Oh, how sweet!" Nat simpers.

"Stop fucking with me. What good did it do? My dad thought I was saved, but I still found a way to go to jail."

I hadn't wanted to talk about this—my dad, my childhood,

my failures—but somehow I still found a way to. Cherif looks me right in the eyes and enunciates clearly, like he'd just purged all the alcohol he'd gulped down from his bloodstream. "Can't do nothing about that, brother. *Maktub*. It is written."

On the way back, I put my arm around Nat and we stagger around looking for a taxi.

"Look, you're a woman and you're in a dress. Get out there on the edge of the sidewalk. It'll be easy then."

"Whatever."

"You're not from Paris."

"So?"

"So you don't know a thing about Paris taxis."

Annoyed, she says, "Fine, but I bet you money it won't make a difference."

"OK, you're on. If I win, you stay with me all morning."

She gives me a defiant stare. I know I'm asking a lot. So does she.

"All right."

Despite a high blood alcohol level, my logic turns out to be flawless. A taxi with its light off stops right in front of her while I linger in the shadows. The driver's just finished his shift but offers to drop her if it's on his way. Of course it's on his way. When he spots me walking up I can see he recognizes the con instantly and regrets ever having stopped. We get in. In the rear-view, his eyes glower, not thrilled that a brown boy like me and a woman as beautiful as Nat are spending the night together.

We kiss on the landing. Once we're in the bed, our ardor flags, and we fall asleep, far too drunk to do a thing.

When I wake up, I realize she hasn't kept her word. Nat's gone, leaving me alone with the mother of all headaches. I get up and realize it won't be long before I throw up, which I do a few minutes later after tossing back a whole glass of water in my kitchen. My forehead's still propped on the toilet seat when I feel my phone vibrating in my pocket. I lift my head and bring a shaky hand to my jeans. I check the caller. Eve?

I probably sound like death warmed over when I pick up. "Hello?"

"Idir?"

"Yes." A beat. "How're things, Eve?"

"Fine, I—I'm with someone who'd like to talk to you. Can we meet up?"

I gauge my hangover. Just appraising it hurts very much. "Oh. I, uh—"

"It's about Thibaut. It's important. Real important."

"OK. I can be over in half an hour."

"Not my place. Meet me in the same café as the first time."

I drag myself over to the shower. When I step out on the street, the light ambushes me. The metro ride is one of the worst I've ever taken—I feel like I'm in a goddamn rowboat off goddamn Cape Horn.

I reach the café. Eve is seated at a table, talking with a young man. I'm glad they're sitting outside. I don't know if I could've stood being indoors amid assholes and their chatter about the latest show at the Cartier-Bresson Foundation. Just then, the waiter drops by and asks me what I want. The thought of a coffee makes me want to puke. A Coke at €5.50 seems like the best money I've ever spent. I order and sit down.

"Idir, this is Arthur."

"Nice to meet you."

They look at each other, embarrassed, like we've got all the time in the world.

"Look, I was out late last night. My head is killing me, and I was planning to spend the day in bed. You look like a sweet kid, but that won't keep me from throwing up all over you if we stay here too long. So say what you have to say, or I'm outta here."

Eve dives in first. "Arthur was...Thibaut's boyfriend. He contacted me last night. Thibaut had told him about me."

Thibaut never mentioned Arthur on the tapes. I turn to him. "Well?"

He makes up his mind to speak at last. His voice sounds worried. I get the feeling he might break out blubbering any minute. "We were supposed to go away together. We'd bought our plane tickets. The day we were supposed to leave, I was going to meet him at the airport but he didn't show up."

"Go where?"

"A little tour around South America."

Poor dumb fucks thought they were adventurers. The kind of guys you'd find wandering around Ciudad Juárez at three in the morning looking for a karaoke bar. I'm thinking it's a good thing this trip never happened. It wouldn't have ended well.

"I haven't heard from him since."

I feel bad for Arthur. He's one of those people who don't believe evil exists. A vast club whose members I keep running into day after day. Always thinking everything's going to work out just fine. They haven't seen what I've seen. Usually when I meet them, they've just gotten booted out on their asses from this fraternity of the gullible and are frantically looking around for an instruction manual that doesn't exist.

"Not a word?" I ask, to be sure he's not hiding anything.

"No." He doesn't sound like he's lying.

"His phone?"

"Voice mail."

"Was he acting funny before you guys were due to leave?"

"He was happy."

"Did he give you the impression he was...seeing someone else?"
He shakes his head.

"Nothing out of the ordinary?"

"He said he felt like he was being followed." He swallows. "He'd been feeling that way for weeks. Then one night, two guys tried to force him into a car on our way back to his place. I screamed, and since there were people around, the two guys drove off."

"You remember what they look like?"

"No, it was dark out."

"Did you report the incident?"

"Yes, but they didn't come up with anything."

Faint alarm bells ring in my head, and I can't blame the hangover. I told Oscar everything would work out because I was sure his brother had up and left to live his life the way he wanted— somewhere free of the assholes who circled like vultures. But if his boyfriend was left waiting at the airport, representing Thibaut's biggest chance at escape, and he didn't show up for it...that put a different spin on things.

"Is that everything?"

He looks at me, wide-eyed. "Isn't that enough?"

I try not to be brusque with him. "I don't work for the cops. Just his brother, who paid me to try and find him. I can't go any further."

"You got your money, so you don't give a shit, is that it?"

"Listen up, you little fuck. If I didn't give a shit I wouldn't be here watching you snivel and listening to your sob story. Got it?"

He looks down, intimidated. "His brother's a bastard. He hated Thibaut. He always kept him at a distance, afraid he'd hurt the family's reputation. The thought that he could benefit even a little from the empire their father left behind drove him crazy. He would've killed him to keep him from getting any of it."

I think back to the press clippings that showed them joined at the hip. And Thibaut's voice on the tapes. I begin to think I've messed up big time, that I've been wrong about everything from the start.

———————————

I go home. Try to reach Nat. Leave her a message saying I had a great time last night and I hope I'll see her again tonight. After which I lie down on the couch for a break. I make like nothing's wrong, but I know I'm trying to fend off guilt. Guilt over botching a case and getting paid off. Guilt over thinking about Nat while a little voice inside me whispers: *You're just a shit. You're sleeping with a married woman—a woman married to your friend. But she'll never be your wife. And—* The voice stops. I'd completely forgotten about the GPS I abandoned on a corner of my dresser—the one I found in the bedroom at the Louasse brothers' house. I unwind the power cord and examine the device. It's in bad shape. There's a hairline crack all the way down the right side of the screen. I lie back down on the couch and press the little button on the side to turn it on. The screen blinks; not much battery left. Mechanically, I press on the icon for recent destinations. They're all in Seine-Saint-Denis, zip code prefix 93, or in Paris. From the list of a dozen or so, only two stick out. One in Boulogne-Billancourt, to the southwest, and the other far out in Seine-et-Marne. I press on the screen again, like I'm actually trying to go to these places. A female voice rings out in the apartment and announces that I am approximately forty-five minutes from my destination. Suddenly, a brief beep and the screen goes dark. No more battery. I could let it go. I figure I'd had enough alcohol yesterday to merit a little siesta right about now. But I pick up my phone again, this time to call Cherif.

"Yeah?"

"I need you, Cherif."

"I'm fucking sleeping!"

"Cherif, I really need you."

"What for?"

"I have to go somewhere. Out in 77, Seine-et-Marne."

He lets out a laugh. "Are you crazy? Come by and grab my car, if you have to, but—"

"You know I don't have a license."

"Then take the bus!"

He hangs up. Can't argue with that.

I lie down on the couch again and tell myself maybe it's better this way. But my phone rings.

"Fuck me, you are such an asshole! I'm awake now. Riquet in half an hour."

Cherif's face is puffy from drinking, lack of sleep, and a bad mood. He hasn't bothered changing out of his tracksuit and a thick cotton sweatshirt before coming out.

"Why'd you bring a GPS?" he asks once I'm in the car. "I have one."

"It's the GPS I found in Bagnolet. There's an address in it I want to visit."

"What do you want to go there for?"

"I'll explain on the way."

"Well, start explaining."

The GPS lets out a long, shrill beep.

"I think the batteries are dead."

"Oh, give it to me!" He grabs the device from my hands and plugs the cord into his lighter. He checks the trip time on the screen and groans at the distance.

"Oh, quit moaning. Don't you want to spend the afternoon with me?"

"I wanted to spend it at home, sleeping."

We exit Paris and head east on the highway. When the GPS tells us to exit, we find ourselves in the middle of the countryside. Soon the pavement runs out and we're heading down a bumpy road. A quick curve to the left and the car finds itself nosed up against a gate.

"End of the road," says Cherif.

"We're not there yet."

"There's nothing fucking here! You see a house or anything? No, just fields. We're going back to Paris."

"Just a sec." I open the door.

"Idir!"

I walk up to the gate, check there's no one around, and step over it.

I pass through a curtain of trees, sink into leaves the rain has reduced to a shapeless mush. The first few drops of sweat start prickling my forehead. After a bender, you tend to sweat more easily. I sponge off my face and keep walking straight ahead. Two minutes later, I see a stone cottage emerge from the trees about fifty yards away. I stop and crouch down, back against a trunk. My legs start trembling and my stomach contracts.

"Where are you?"

I hear Cherif's voice. He's just passed through the curtain of trees. I hiss at him and hold a finger up to my lips. He comes over silently. I whisper, "There's a cottage over there."

"Where?"

I point left. He looks.

No sign of life around. The only window we can see on this side is tiny and too filthy to afford a glimpse through.

"I want to find out what's inside."

He reaches behind him and pulls a gun from his waistband.

"I didn't like feeling naked in front of that ski-masked asshole with a gun last time. Go ahead, I'll cover you."

Bent over, I run to the cottage and flatten myself against the wall right by the door.

I wave Cherif over. He takes up a position on the other side of the door. I signal one, two, three. He kicks the door right by the knob and it gives way.

It's empty. And dirty. One room with a mattress on the dirt floor, a Thermos, empty Coke bottles, a plastic baggie full of weed, and beer bottles turned into ashtrays, the necks whitened by cinder.

"Smells like your mom," Cherif mutters.

I grimace. The shut-in smell, on top of stale tobacco and damp rot, is harder to take than Cherif's joke.

"See? Nothing here. Can we go now?"

We go.

"Wait." I decide to walk around the cottage. Nothing except for a shovel against one wall.

"See? Not a damn thing."

Absently, I grab the shovel. *Think, think*. There are too many threads all tangled up in my mind. I'm not smart enough to pick them all apart. It annoys me. I swing the shovel against the wall. Again and again, harder each time, until my arm muscles start burning. Like the *klong* the metal makes on stone might clear my head. The soil on the shovel comes off and splatters on the limewash wall, a leech the color of clay, and—blood. I scratch at the muddy leavings. The dirt is red in places. I start running around the cottage, looking everywhere.

"Idir, you wanna tell me what's going on?"

"The shovel!"

"The shovel what?"

"I—I think there's blood on it."

"You sure?"

"I think."

"It could be anything, you know."

But I'm already far afield. I'm walking without really knowing where I'm going, trudging in circles. Until, about thirty yards from the house, I find a pile of fresh earth.

"Cherif, bring the shovel."

He hands it over. "What do you think is under there?"

I don't say anything, just start digging. They didn't do a very good job. The hole isn't very deep. A few shovelfuls later, I hit something. A man's hand comes out of the ground.

"Oh, fuck!"

I jump back. Cherif too.

"What the fuck is this?"

I keep digging. The smell becomes hard to take. A bloated belly shows next, crisscrossed with swollen veins, gleaming purplish streaks about to break through the translucent skin. Then a face. Hard to believe it was once alive, that it was once a man's. It looks like a mask, something out of a movie. Except I know this face. I've seen it before, in photos. Smiling.

"It's Thibaut," I say.

"Who?"

"The kid I was looking for."

"The fuck's he doing here?"

I take out my phone.

"What are you doing?"

"Calling the cops. You can go home, Cherif."

Cherif puts a hand on my arm. "What are you, stupid? What are you going to tell them?"

"That I found this body by accident."

"The fuck is a guy like you doing way the fuck out here? You're from the city. You've got no business out here in a field. Your prints are on the shovel and all over the place.

"What the fuck do you want me to do?"

He hands me the car keys. "Go to the car. Call your client and tell him the news. I'll clean up here and then we go home. As for the cops, we wait. It won't change anything. This guy is dead; he's not going anywhere. We'll see what happens after."

I do as he says and walk back to the car in a daze. I stumble and fall, pick myself back up. I can't manage to throw up, though I want to. I stick two fingers down my throat to get the retching started. But all my empty belly turns up is some acid bile, which I swallow back down painfully.

I shut myself in the car, happy for a refuge far from the kid. I dial the number right away, so I don't have time to think twice. He picks up quick.

"Idir?"

"I have some news about your brother—"

He doesn't let me finish. His voice is full of hope. "You found him?"

"Yeah."

"Well?"

"I don't know how to say this, so I'll just say it straight up: he's dead."

I hear a swallowing sound, then silence.

"You still there?"

"Yes."

"Let's meet. I don't like phone calls." I hang up. Cherif comes back a few minutes later. He starts the car.

"What do you think?" he asks.

"I have no idea, Cherif. No idea." I start hitting the dashboard again and again. "I don't fucking understand any of this bullshit!"

"Those two brothers must've done it. They're dead; justice is served. Doesn't happen often, so don't beat yourself up over it."

"Why'd they kidnap him?"

"It's what they do."

"Yeah, but why him?"

"His family's loaded. That not enough reason for you?"

"Cherif, you don't get it. I was asked to find the kid. I couldn't do it. Then some other guy asks me to find his car. And the guys who stole the car are also mixed up with the kid. One client's problem is bleeding into another client's bigger problem. Coincidence?" I shake my head. "No way. It just doesn't add up."

"Those guys were degenerates. They're not out there planning for retirement. They kidnap people, OK? But then they saw the car, so they took it. Because they felt like it, the way you feel like you need to take a leak all of a sudden. They saw a shitload of money rolling by, and so fuck the consequences."

"So why kill the kid, then? How'd they know his family was rich? It doesn't hold up."

"Look, he's dead. It's sad, but that's how it is. Now they're dead, and they deserved what they got. For fuck's sake, let it go. Forget it!"

"What would they get out of killing him? Tell me that."

"Maybe he just mouthed off to them, Idir, or they woke up one morning wondering what would happen if they killed him.

There's no fucking telling."

I know something's wrong here, and I doubt I can figure it out. "Cherif, coincidence is for normal law-abiding citizens. You believe in coincidence in your line of work?"

"What now?"

"If some guy makes you steal a car and the next morning the cops kick in your door, you'd figure he'd turned you in, right?"

"Well, sure."

"So you don't believe in coincidence."

"No."

"So we agree. It's all connected."

I don't know why I insisted on seeing Oscar in person. As if it were going to change anything. But I need to know more because suddenly these families are connected.

Oscar greets me very solemnly, as if he has to keep his sadness from me. It hasn't hit him yet; he still hopes I'm wrong. Or at least that's what it seems like. "Are you sure it was him?"

"I think it's him."

"You could've made a mistake?" he asks in a voice full of hope. I can't bring myself to contradict him.

"Yes. Anyone can make a mistake."

"Where'd you find him?"

"Far from here. Out in the country."

"Can you take me there? I'd know if it was him."

"We're talking about a body, you know. I'd rather notify the police first. That'd be the straight thing to do. They can notify you after."

"If that really is my brother out there, you'd be a key witness in the trial."

"Look, you paid me for my work, I did it. If you mention my name so much as once in the police investigation, I'll deny everything."

He pauses only for a moment, like my reply doesn't really matter. "So it's him, huh?"

I swallow. "It's the same face as in the photo."

He stifles a sob and lets out a little keening sound. "Sorry, sorry, I'm just a bit...shaken. You did good work though."

"I'll call the police from a pay phone. Just an anonymous tip. The rest is out of my hands."

"Thanks for everything."

I give him a wave and head for the door. I can already see myself outside, taking in a big breath of fresh air. But his voice rings out behind me. "I know who the real culprit is, even if he'll never be caught."

I turn around. He comes up to me and says, "And so do you. Eric Vernay."

His voice has changed. I don't like it. I'm starting to feel like a mute extra in some scene of Oscar's devising. "I'm not covering for anyone. Not him, not you. Your affairs don't concern me."

"Listen—I got my hands on lots of compromising documents related to his company. Enough to cause a scandal. A big one. I was counting on revealing the information. All of a sudden my brother disappears, and one day, I get a phone call. It was him. He was sobbing. I could hear voices behind him. He begged me to come get him, said he didn't want to die. And then—*click*."

"Why didn't you tell me?"

He gives me a disillusioned smile, the better to hide the tears welling up in his eyes. "Oh, I don't know—I didn't know if you were still close to Vernay. I—I don't know."

I begrudge him for not playing it straight with me, for not putting me in the know right from the start. I might've been able to save the kid.

"Why didn't you alert the police?"

"I was scared—for him."

"You think Vernay's behind all this?"

"Who else?"

"You have proof?"

"Nothing. You have more proof than I do. In truth, you're the only one with any proof. And if I understood you correctly, you don't wish to testify."

I can't meet his gaze. "I don't work for Eric, and I have nothing to do with his schemes."

He hesitates, stares intently at me for a minute, scouring the depths of my soul. "I believe you—and I respect your decision."

"It's my job. I can't get involved in all the rest. We had a contract, I held up my end. How doesn't matter. I swear I have no information about whoever did this. You'll have to take my word for it, because that's all I'll give you."

Since the two brothers are dead, I figure the truth won't help anyone, just hurt him.

"I understand. Thanks for all your help, at any rate. Thanks for not giving up."

"I'll call the police—about the location. Call them yourself after that and report your brother missing. It'll be some time before they identify the body. Good luck with all the rest."

"I hope—I hope you were wrong. That it wasn't him."

"Me too."

I go home to give myself some room to think in peace. Later, I'll go find a pay phone and place the call. When I get my keys out on the landing, I hear footsteps behind me in the stairwell. I pay no attention and open my door. That's when a hand squeezes my shoulder with a bone-crushing grip and shoves me inside the apartment.

His face says a lot about him: his nose must've been broken lots of time, his high cheekbones hide dark little half-shut eyes, his fat cheeks are swollen from old punches. He's not far from six feet and seems in good shape—the kind of guy who'll catch up if you try to run away. The fact that he's letting me see his face is not a good sign. He pulls a gun. I wonder if he's going to put a bullet in my head and leave me bleeding on the floor. I'll just be the second guy that happened to in this apartment. The truth is I'm shitting bricks and don't want history to repeat itself. Especially since, against a guy like him, I've got no chance.

"Mr. Vernay would like to see you."

That accent. Mr. Ski Mask.

The car is double-parked—a black German sedan. Not the same model as last time. It's like they have a whole collection. I catch the driver's eyes in the rearview. About as comforting as those of his partner, who's gotten in next to me to make sure I behave. No point asking questions. I already know where we're going and why. I prefer silence. It helps me concentrate on the plan I'll have to come up with before we get there. I have one thing on my side: he doesn't know where Thibaut's body is. Or else I'd be dead already. It's my only leverage against him. I'm relieved when I see the car take the route I expect.

He welcomes me into his big apartment with a view of the Eiffel Tower, where I used to come as a kid for the parties Thomas would throw when his dad wasn't around, with all-you-can-drink champagne.

"Leave us alone."

The goon obeys. He hasn't said a word since my apartment. He vanishes without a sound—two hundred pounds moving in perfect silence. Eric's sitting in an armchair.

"Sit down."

"I like standing."

He gets up. For the first time, I see him as someone who can't stand not having everything in his control. "Sorry to bring you over so late. But I think you're smart enough to know why you're here."

I don't answer. He goes on. "You see, my boy, some things are just above your head. I'm not here to explain them all, much less justify myself. You don't become what I am without giving up a few things of a...moral nature."

He trips up a little over these last words, like they're not quite what he means but he can't find better ones. "But let's say all this went off the rails. I didn't want certain information to slip out. The company's not doing very well. So the last thing I need is bad press."

He snickers to himself. "I entrusted the affair to some small-timers, so they couldn't trace it back to me. I figured Oscar would be smart enough to figure out that it wasn't a coincidence—that his brother had been kidnapped, and it was no accident."

"So you had his brother kidnapped and you called to tell him to back off?"

"I never called him. I wanted him to figure it out on his own. I had to remain invisible, or else I would've had my own men do it. It was just a warning. A week or two. He'd know what I was capable of. I wanted to frighten him, that's all. But the shit hit the fan and believe me, I'm sorry."

At no moment does it seem to have occurred to him that Oscar might have refused to back down. That his brother's kidnapping might only have stiffened his resolve.

"You should've been more careful with your human resources. For a CEO, that's a big oversight."

He smiles, like he knows my remark hides the phony composure of a TV hero.

"Exactly, my boy, exactly. I hired a pair of incompetents. That they were ultraviolent didn't help. The brothers were supposed to keep the boy, not kill him. I sent my men to check on them. They were supposed to give proof of life and all that in exchange for a payment. Then sit tight. Instead, those morons stole the car. They took the money and the car and kept the kid. We managed to catch up with one of the brothers. The other one took it on the lam. I don't know what happened after that. You found the car—I think that was enough to cover me. I distanced myself from the rest. I thought they'd let the boy go. But today he calls me up—Mr. Great Media Tycoon, my ass— and tells me he knows where his brother died." He scoffs at the whole fiasco, then goes serious again. "I just want to know where he is. I'll pay."

He pauses for a moment, checks my reaction. I have no idea what my face betrays.

"So that's why you hired me. Once Thomas blurted that I was working for Crumley, you thought I might prove useful in the long run. Very inspired of you—"

"I may be a lot of things, but I'm no murderer. All you have to do is give me a figure and an address."

"You're going to send your men in to clean up, is that it? No body, no charges. Trouble is I don't know where he is."

"I don't believe you."

"This is where you start threatening me, right? Telling me how your bodyguards were mixed up in some ugly shit back in Eastern Europe or wherever, that kind of bullshit. But they can work me over with a blowtorch, it won't change a thing. I didn't find him. I told Crumley I was giving up. It's been two weeks. It never occurred to you he might try to bluff, to do you one better?"

"No. Because I know when people are bluffing. That's why I'm going to be square with you. I'm going to let you go home and sleep on it. Sleep hard. Come up with a figure. And tomorrow, you can come back and we'll pick up our little conversation where we left off."

"And if I refuse?"

"You're within your rights. I won't hurt you." He notes the surprise on my face. He goes on. "But as for Nathalie, well...Oh, please, don't look so surprised. I know about you two. You really think I'm that stupid? I even have photos. You like that, when she sucks your cock?"

"You're a psychopath—"

"You like her. I don't. So go off somewhere, the both of you, with my money. I know you want to. And I'd be happy to give it to you."

―――――――――――

The ride home is even worse, stuck in back with the big goon again. I picture the possibility of skipping town with Nathalie and the money. It's tempting, but thoughts of Thibaut distract me. With the goon not taking his eyes off me, I close my own to pay Thibaut a visit in the underworld. To tell him why justice will never be done. I owe him that much, a ghostly conversation a few minutes long, and then I'm out of there with a clear conscience. Right by the shallow grave where his corpse lies, unearthed by my frenzied digging, I whisper, "Better give up on a gravestone, buddy."

"Who are you?"

"Your brother hired me to find you."

"My brother? I have no brother."

"Oscar."

"He doesn't give a damn about me."

"He's an asshole, I know, I listened to the tapes. But you're wrong, kid, he was sad when I told him you were dead."

"He's a good actor. Where is he?"

"He won't be coming."

"Why?"

"I can't tell anyone you're here. Nothing personal, pal. But you're already dead, so—"

"Can I get a coffin? It's cold here."

I take off my coat and spread it over him. "Here. It's all I have."

"Thanks. Now leave me alone, if that's all you have to tell me. Talking with you has worn me out. I'd like to rest now."

"You hold it against me?"

But he's already fallen silent. He's underground. And he's told me what I have to do.

A hand pressing down on my shoulder jerks me from my reverie. The gorilla looks at me, no expression on his face. "We're here."

I look out the window and recognize my neighborhood.

"You have kids?" I ask him before I get out.

"No," he replies, simple as that.

"You want any?"

"No."

"I know, right? World we live in."

He grunts. I open the door, thinking that's all I'll get out of him.

"My sister had one. Cops gunned him down. I think that's what changed my mind," he finally says.

I get out of the car, convinced his eyes are trained on my back when I open the door to my building.

As soon as I get in, I call Cherif. He picks up right away.

"I really need some help this time."

"What else is new?"

My phone rings again a few hours later. It's Nat, panicked. "I have to see you right away."

I can tell from her voice she's not doing so well. "What's wrong?"

She bursts into tears. "I was attacked."

I take her to the ER at Lariboisière. Just another Saturday night by Gare du Nord: several junkies in withdrawal talking to themselves between screams; a guy cuffed to the radiator, flanked by SWAT in ski masks; and another guy, drunk—it's unclear if his nose was busted in a fight or if he did it himself pitching face-forward on the sidewalk. The list goes on. The down-and-out of every stripe, living a life in name only. And Nat, her eyes filled with tears, two fingers broken. For the tenth time, I make her tell me what happened.

She was going downstairs in her building when a guy came out of the elevator and hit her. Then he leaned over her, undid her belt. She pushed him back; he broke her fingers. Then he changed his mind, smiled, and whispered in her ear, "I know that got you wet."

"What did he look like?"

"I don't know. I can't remember. He had an Eastern European accent."

"And he didn't take anything?"

"No."

"And you're not pressing charges?"

"What?"

"You don't want your husband to find out, is that it?"

She peeks at me out of the corner of her eye. "Stop judging me."

"I'm not judging. I'm trying to help you."

"Sorry."

I get out of my seat. "Wait here, just let me check on something."

I head for reception and ask the woman who's tapping on her keyboard behind the counter, "How much longer will we have to wait?"

She lifts her head, looks at me. She's got bags under her eyes, and her makeup is cracked here and there. She brushes a lock of hair—a bad red dye job—back behind her ear and sighs. I wonder how many times she's heard the same question over the decade or two she's worked here, forget about just today.

"You have a number, sir. We'll call you when it's your turn."

After two hours of waiting, our number finally comes up. The doctor asks her what happened. She tells him she fell. He gives me the *look*. Clearly, I'm the one who broke her fingers— out of jealousy, because I was drunk or the soup was cold. I don't blame him. He must see lots of cases like this. That look is his only retaliation, his only way of making people who do such things know they're bastards. Or maybe I'm making things up and he doesn't give a damn.

"I'm going to give you a temporary splint while we wait for the X-ray." The doctor positions the splint around her fingers, bandages them up, then points us to another room. "Wait here, they'll come get you for the X-ray."

With these words, he strolls away without so much as a wave. I offer Nat a seat, but she refuses.

"C'mon, Idir, we're going."

"What about the X-ray?"

"I'll do it tomorrow near my place."

I don't have time to insist; she's already walking off.

It's cold now outside. I offer her my jacket. She refuses.

"Can I walk you back?"

"I'd like to go to your place," she says without looking at me.

I bring her back home. I kiss her wrist, slip her maimed fingertips, which stick out past the splint, into my mouth. We make love, slowly. Afterward, we fall asleep, sadder than when we came in.

The next day, I wake up beside her. "I thought you'd be gone already."

"I needed to stay this morning." She kisses my brow.

"Want some coffee?"

She smiles. "I thought you'd never ask."

I get dressed quick and dash to the kitchen. While the coffeemaker warms up, I send Cherif a text message: "Get ready."

I don't hear her come into the kitchen. "What are you doing?"

"Nothing. It was Cherif. I have to meet up with him later."

She comes over to me, puts her head on my shoulder, and whispers in my ear, "Thank you. Thanks for being there."

We sit down on the sofa when the coffee's done. I still don't know what to think of her. She takes a gulp in silence and I watch her, as if that might be enough to sort everything out.

"You know, maybe you and I, we should give it a shot."

I thought I was lost, but suddenly, here's a sign. Not much, just one tiny little sentence. But now I know. I know; I'm sure. A few minutes later, I kiss her on the doorstep. I think she says, "See you tonight," but I'm not listening anymore.

I go back to my living room and jump on the phone. "You in place?"

"Yeah," says Cherif.

"She's coming down."

"We're good. I'll call you back."

Right or wrong. I don't know which I'd rather be. Or I do. I'd rather be right, to give something back to the kid. Not justice. I'm not up to that. And who am I to judge? Just a friendly helping hand. That'd be good already.

The wait is too long. I hit redial on my phone.

"Yeah? What now? I told you I'd keep you updated!"

"Where is she?"

"Trocadéro."

"She could be going to see him. Or she could just as easily be going home."

"That's why I said I'd call you."

"I need this real-time."

"Goddammit, you're such a pain in the ass. Fine."

A few seconds of silence.

"Well?"

"She's headed home."

"You sure?"

"If you gave me the right address, then yes."

At that moment, I'm relieved. To be wrong about her.

"The taxi's double-parked, hazards on."

"I was totally wrong."

"You sound almost happy about it, like it suits you."

I don't answer. Now I'm on my own.

"So what do we do now?"

"I don't know, Cherif."

"You can't bring that kid back to life. It's not your fight. That woman's amazing; don't put her in danger. Think about her"— he pauses—"and you."

"I have to find—"

"There's nothing to find. And nothing to understand."

"I thought I'd seen through her."

"Idir, you can't see for shit. Were you even there the night of my party?"

"You talked with her for two hours. You don't know her."

"I saw her talking with Momo for half an hour. That guy freaks even me out! You know many babes like that?"

"Cherif, I'm telling you—"

"Your face."

"You can't talk with—"

"I said shut your face, she's turning around."

"What?"

"The taxi's making a U-turn. Goddammit! Shit!"

I hear a brief crackling, like the phone's fallen. Then nothing. I call him back, but he doesn't pick up. Once. Twice. Three times—

"Yeah."

"Fuck, Cherif! Well?"

"She's at his place. Just went up. You were right."

———————

Oscar looks in better shape than the night before. At least before he spots me and meets my eyes. He gives me a sad little smile and waves me over.

"Sorry to bother you."

"You're not bothering me at all."

"I'd've liked to have told you where the body was earlier, but I had to cover my tracks."

He doesn't reply.

"You thought I was Eric's man, is that it? You were convinced I never learned a thing, after all these years. That I can always be bought."

"No. I think you're someone who's loyal. You came to find me before he did. You didn't give up looking. I thought he'd threatened you and you were afraid—only natural, given the kind of man he is."

"I had to make sure he couldn't touch me."

"And now you're sure?"

I don't answer his question. No one's ever sure of anything; we just hope it'll be enough. "I think I owe you the whole story. Once more, I still won't testify. But I'll tell you everything. Eric came to see me shortly after you did. He'd had a luxury car stolen. He wanted to find it. I found the thieves, two brothers, who did all sorts of nasty stuff to pay their rent. They were the ones who kidnapped your brother. On Eric's orders—he must've used a middleman, to be sure it wouldn't be traced back to him. Those were undoubtedly the same two brothers who killed Thibaut before being mysteriously killed themselves. I found one with a bullet in his head at his own house. There was also a GPS there. I went to one of the addresses on it. That's where I found your brother. They dumped him in a shallow grave out in a field."

He takes this in, jaw tight.

"I don't know if this'll make you feel better, but the two guys are dead. I think the deal went bad. They got too greedy and got their own ideas, except their own ideas weren't so bright. At any rate, they stole Eric's car and took Thibaut with them. I think Eric hired a killer to take care of it, and that's when it all went off the rails. Thibaut really was just stuck in the middle."

"That son of a bitch is going to pay. There's nothing holding me back now. I'll reveal it all. But he won't ever stand trial for my brother's death, especially if you refuse to testify." He watches me, like he's seeing if I'll change my mind.

"I sympathize, but I won't testify. Judge me if you want, but that's not part of my job or our agreement." I restrain myself from telling him about the other brother, the one I pummeled into oblivion on Thibaut's behalf.

"I understand. It's just—"

Tears spring to his eyes. I try to explain.

"Whether I testify or not won't change a thing. No matter what happens, guys like that will never go to jail. Do your work and bury your brother. That'll be enough already. Got a pen?"

After my meeting with Oscar, I dash out on the Champs-Élysées and call Eric.

"Ah, at last. I thought you'd never make up your mind."

I contrive a panicked voice. "I'll tell you everything on one condition—don't hurt Nat anymore."

"You know I didn't enjoy that. I'm listening."

I give him the address where Thibaut lies peacefully. Suddenly I sort of regret it all. The disruption that's coming for the dead kid. But it's the best I can do. I figure Eric's men will head over there right away to look for the body, which gives me a little more than an hour. So I decide to walk over—it's one of the few free pleasures left in Paris. Might as well enjoy it.

Eric's secretary starts getting upset at the sight of my face. This time I don't even stop for her, just push the door right open. She starts screaming.

"Sir, you can't do that! I'm calling security!"

I enter the office. Eric is by the window, phone to his ear. He sees me come in, followed by his horrified secretary, and realizes something's up. A fleeting moment of doubt passes over his face. Then he regains control.

"It's all right, Brigitte."

She tries to make an excuse. "But, sir—"

"Just close the door behind you."

She obeys, giving me a dark look as she exits.

"I thought we were square."

I look at him, grinning. "Your men not answering?"

"Excuse me?"

"The big gorilla who brought me here last time. I'm sure he's not answering." I wait to make sure that's the case. Eric flexes his jaw. Then I plunge in: "Want to know why? Because the cops arrested him. I told Oscar where his brother's body was. I also told him I'd never testify in the case. But that didn't keep me from giving him a little helping hand. I give you the address. You send your man. The police and your man probably had a nice little meet and greet. Now we'll see if he's a good little soldier. If the cops toss life at him, will he still be that loyal?"

Eric shakes his head, like he doesn't understand what I've just told him. Then he pulls himself together. "You'll regret this. You were warned."

"Oh yeah? More threats about Nat? Let me tell you something. I know she was in on it. I know the attack was bullshit. I followed her after she left my place; she went straight to yours, probably to tell you the plan was working, that I was scared to death for her. The problem, the only problem, is that you took me for an idiot."

"Why'd you do this? For that kid? You didn't even know him."

"Because I was paid to find him."

"You wanted to play the hero, is that it? The righter of wrongs." He starts laughing, a little nervous laugh that turns into a coughing fit.

"What's the matter?"

"I sure got hoodwinked on this one. Remarkable," he adds, as if to himself, staring into the distance. Then he straightens up and looks at me. "You still never got it. You were focused on me. You're not used to this kind of fight."

"You played and lost. That's all."

"Yes, I lost. But so did you. Oscar screwed you over, just like he screwed me. Think about one thing, Idir: Who profits from this crime? I stood to gain nothing from the kid's death. What counted for me was having him alive. So ask yourself: Why did the two brothers keep him and kill him?"

Too late. It's over. I don't want to hear anymore.

I'm barely out of the building when my phone rings. It's Cherif. "You watching the news?"

"No."

"It's over. They found the body. They also say they've arrested a suspect." Cherif chuckles heartily. "I wonder if that asshole was wearing a ski mask when he showed up."

Cherif's in a good mood. "We celebrating this with a drink?"

I don't feel like it, but I don't see myself going home and acting like nothing's the matter either. "Sure, but we're getting hammered."

————————————

It's four o'clock when I throw up for the first time, on a bench in square Léon. Vomit falls on my shoes. I don't know how many bottles of beer I've tossed back on that bench. Cherif is having a grand old time. Until I keel over. I feel hands on me. Hands of the homeless people from square Léon—with purplish joints and skin eaten away by injections that have tripled the size of their fingers—grabbing me and setting me back on my feet.

"Can you walk?"

Cherif's voice seems to come from very far away. I say yes. He lets me go. I fall again.

"Right, I see."

They all pick me up again.

"I'll go get the car. All I ask is don't puke inside."

I have the decency to open the door at a red light and puke on the pavement. "Goddamn, Idir—!"

He goes back and forth between reprimands and bursts of laughter. "Man, you hung one the fuck on!"

"Shut your face," I say. "I feel like shit."

"I've never seen you looking this lily-white before. A perfect little Frenchman."

Sometime later, I'm looking up into his face.

"You should go see your banker. This is probably the only day of your life he'll ever approve a loan."

He laughs at his shitty joke. I close my eyes, trying to keep the nausea at bay.

———————

In the stairwell. My arm slung around Cherif's shoulders.
"Hang on, we're almost there...Keys? Where are they?"
"Pocket."
The old neighbor lady looks away when she passes.
"We're fine, madame—he's just a little under the weather."
In the time it takes him to fumble around in my pocket, I fall to the floor. He leaves me there and opens the door.
He sticks a hand out. "C'mon, just a little further."
"Leave me here. I'll go inside when I feel better."
"Idir, you can't just lie here on your doormat."
"No, I...I have to think."
"You're wasted."
"Just leave me alone!"
"Fine. Call me when you're better." He doesn't insist, just hands me my keys and leaves me lying there in front of the wide-open door to my apartment.

———————

I let my numb finger rest on the doorbell. I've managed to drag myself here after sleeping for an hour on my doormat. If she's inside, she'll either open up or call the cops. I hear footsteps. Then silence. A brief pause to peer out through the peephole.
"It's me. Open up, goddammit."
Not a sound. I know she's behind that goddamned door, wondering what to do.

"You might not feel better once we've talked, but I will. I think you owe me at least that much." I hear the dead bolt slide in the lock. Then there she is, impeccably made up, bright red lips, in a big sweater that hangs halfway down her thighs, sheathed in black stockings.

"What are you doing here? If Thomas knew—"

I wedge my foot in the doorway. "Stop treating me like a moron. I know full well he's not here. He's in New York."

She tries to close the door, but too late, I'm already inside.

"You're crazy."

I look at her.

"You've been drinking," she adds, scowling with disgust.

I give her my wickedest smile on top of my acid breath.

"What do you want?"

"To know."

"You know everything."

"No, I don't think so. I want to know what you got out of it. If you were in on it right from the start, or if he manipulated you somehow."

"He found out about us. He had photos. He threatened to show them to Thomas."

"So what?"

"I'm over thirty, Idir. I'm not a girl anymore. I have to think about—"

"Your life in the high tower, huh? Is that it?"

"No, it's not. It's just I recently found out—"

"Found out you liked money. That this piece-of-shit life was right up your alley. That you were ready to throw me over for this apartment, these paintings on the wall, and the rest of that bullshit. You don't even realize. I was afraid Eric would hurt you. And here you come, with tears in your eyes—"

"You have no idea what this cost—"

I grab her bandaged hand and squeeze. "Here's what it cost."

"Stop it! You're hurting me."

"Here's what it cost. Two broken fingers to make me think you'd been assaulted. You're no better than they are, no better than father or son."

She's weeping now. In a soft voice, she says, "You're right, Idir. You're always right."

She turns on her heel and escapes down the hallway, leaving me standing there in the foyer of her vast apartment.

CHAPTER 7

A WEEK GOES BY. ALONE AT HOME. BLINDS DRAWN FROM noon on. A quick walk around the neighborhood because I can't sleep past five, but then I go back to sleep. I'm out cold three-quarters of the time to keep from thinking. I'm constantly tired, like I'm eating *majoun* for breakfast every day. I come out when night falls. Make myself TV dinners of fries and malt liquor. I'm living the dream. I can't stop thinking about Eric's question, his last words to me: *Why did the two brothers keep him and kill him?*

The Louasse brothers, who decided to double cross Eric in the end, to take the money for the kidnapping job without handing over the kid—the R8 was a bonus. Maybe they finally decided to get rid of the kid when he became too much trouble. Given the personalities of those two psychopaths, it wasn't out of the question. But what if they'd decided to play both sides? If they'd reached out to Oscar and demanded a ransom? No more reason to get rid of Thibaut—unless Oscar had paid the kidnappers not to give his brother back, but to kill him. I can't get it out of my head. I keep mulling it over nonstop, about the fact that I'll never know what really happened, and I can't quite gauge the part I played in all this, how responsible I am for everything that went down. After all, dead people could give a fuck about being avenged.

The eighth day, at nightfall, I go over to my grandmother's. I know wiser people, but they haven't been through as much, at least not in the same way. She still might wind up burying me someday, scrape by and survive the extinction of the human race itself, even the destruction of the entire world. So I decided a few years ago to always listen to what she had to say.

"I was out for a stroll nearby, so I thought I'd stop and say hi."

From the mischievous glint in her eyes, I know she knows I'm lying. As if she knows nothing coming from me is ever sincere.

"Come in, come in. I was making a meal for Aziz."

"Oh—"

"Don't worry, he won't be over right away."

I follow her to the kitchen, sit down, and watch her cutting vegetables.

"You don't look so great."

"I've been asking myself some questions. Doing a little soul-searching."

"Really? You, the know-it-all, asking yourself questions! Now I've seen it all!"

"What about grandfather?"

She gives me a weird look, like bringing up her late husband makes her jumpy right away.

"What about him?"

"You think he was a good man?"

"I don't judge. I'm not God."

"And Dad?"

"I can't judge him either; he's my son."

I smile.

"Would you hate me if I went back to prison?"

She stops a moment, gives me the stink eye of a village witch. "Yes. Why are you asking these questions? Did you do something stupid?"

I refuse to answer and smile instead.

"Are you about to?"

She gives me another hard stare, making it clear that she won't ask a third time, that I have to tell her the truth now.

"No, no, don't worry. It was a dumb question. Forget it."

"You know, Idir, you think the whole world's against you, that you can't lead a normal life, but I don't know what you're waiting for. You young people look down on us, like you're worth more. Like you invented the world. There's more than one way of living a life, of having a good time. But there's only one way to be happy. And if you refuse it, don't take it out on other people, or on God."

I give her a hug. "You're the only woman who puts up with me. I don't know how you do it."

She gives me a good long hug in return. "Oh, it's not as hard as all that."

Eric's name is all over the papers. All they're talking about is beryllium oxide, public housing, a political-financial health scandal. I keep mulling over our conversation. I rewind the tape in my head and think he's right at least about one thing. I *am* the biggest dumb fuck on the planet.

It smells like last things. Cheap Médoc and disgusting food. The wheelchair I'm pushing slides smoothly over the linoleum. I knock before entering. He's reading the paper, glasses perched at the end of his nose.

"Mr. Crumley?"

"Where's Martin?" His voice is still full of vigor.

"He's sick. I'm filling in for him today."

I've prepped my speech. I plan to tell him I'm new, that it's my first week on the job. But he doesn't ask any more questions. So I go over and pick him up. He lets me. It takes me two tries to get him settled in the wheelchair—the man's still heavy.

He remains silent until we reach the garden. I look around for a quiet corner, off to the side, where I can ask my questions undisturbed.

"What do you want?"

The question surprises me.

"I'm perfectly aware you don't work here," he adds, to dissuade me from lying again.

I stop the wheelchair by a bench and sit down. "Your son Oscar hired me to find Thibaut."

He blinks instinctively, though his eyes stay dry.

"So you're the one who found him." His gaze, full of contempt, settles on me. As if I were to blame for what happened to his son. "You should leave now. You have no business here."

He pivots his wheelchair. I grab the wheel with my hand, gripping it as tightly as I can, giving him no choice.

"I don't want to believe there was a link between my brother's death and the revelations." Oscar's playing the dignified victim on every channel. He has refused any police escort. He knows he has nothing to fear now. He passes for a hero; his success is complete. I've been tracking his movements for several weeks now. I know that Thursday night he leaves work early, around late afternoon, to meet up with a young poli-sci student with big tits that look natural, as far as I can tell through my binoculars. I've been watching husbands cheat on their wives and vice versa for a while now, and unlike most, he doesn't fuck her at a hotel. He fucks her on the top floor of an apartment building on rue des Saints-Pères, as if he can feel himself becoming a student again when he jumps her bones on the little sofa bed in that garret.

There's an apartment for sale on the third floor. It's empty. I had time to get a double of the keys made thanks to a slim metal shank sheathed in modeling clay. I've also brought a gun, the one Claude Louasse pointed at my face, the .45 with flaking paint.

I hurry into the building behind him; he glances briefly at me while holding the door. I thank him. The visor of the baseball cap pulled low over my eyes keeps him from recognizing me, unless it's that his imagination's already preoccupied by his girlfriend's breasts.

There's no elevator, which makes things easier. I let him start up the stairs. He goes up, whistling. One flight. *The best part of love is when you're going up the stairs.* Who said that? Can't remember anymore. Two flights. He's about to start up the next flight when I charge across the landing, take aim, and smack him right between the shoulder blades. His head smashes into the wall. He hits the ground, totally dazed. I use these precious seconds to open the door to the empty apartment. I drag him in by the sleeve while he's groaning. I shut the door. Alone at last. The apartment is spacious and bathed in bright white light. I take off the baseball cap and toss it at him. He starts blinking.

"Idir? Goddamn, Idir, it is you. What the hell are you doing?"

"You fucked me over."

"What are you talking about? Have you lost it?" He brings a hand to his forehead. "Fuck, I'm bleeding!"

I draw my gun.

"Cut it out, don't do something stupid—"

"Shut your face!"

I bury the tip of my shoe in his liver. He lets out a hiss, like he's spitting something out.

"The only one who had anything to gain from things getting worse was you. Eric's a piece of shit, but Thibaut was only valuable to him alive. I paid a visit to your dad at the hospital. He was leaving half his shares to your brother." I wipe the sweat from my brow, realize he's not looking at me anymore, just the gun. "Thibaut told his kidnappers he came from a rich family who'd pay for his freedom. So the Louasse brothers wanted to play both sides. They called you and demanded ransom for your brother. So you paid up—but to have him killed. That way, Daddy's money would be all yours. Eric's biggest mistake in this whole mess? Not knowing who your brother's worst enemy was."

He doesn't answer. I rack the slide. He hears the noise and must be picturing the round entering the chamber.

"Stop it! Put that fucking thing away! Please!"

I lower the weapon.

"I didn't do anything. All I did was tell them that I wouldn't pay. That they'd go to jail."

I forgot for a moment he was a coward, that he'd never be able to make a call like that, that he wouldn't want to get his hands dirty.

"You knew they'd kill him! You wanted to push them to it and cover your tracks."

"I was just testing it out, to see. It could've worked; I wasn't sure. I didn't do anything wrong. It was just bad luck."

"You fucked me over—"

"No. I paid you for your time. You did all the rest. You're the one who wanted to play the white knight. I had nothing to do with it. Nothing."

I bring the gun to his forehead. He keeps his eyes down and lets out a little "no," almost like a nervous breath. A few seconds of dead time before I stick the gun back in my belt and pick up my baseball cap.

"Pleasure working with you," he mutters after me as I go through the door.

I don't look back.

In the metro, my phone rings. It's Thomas. I hesitate to pick up—then figure I'm not afraid. He has a right to know. If he asks, I'll give him a straight answer: his father's a murderer and I fucked his wife.

"Hello?"

"Idir, how's it going?" He sounds happy.

"Never better. You?"

"Great! I have some big news."

"What's that?"

"I'm going to be a dad!"

———————

The bar's noisy, everyone knocking drinks back nonstop. I spot a merry Cherif way in the rear. He gives me a wave and we go out the back door. By the trash cans, he lights a cigarette.

"How'd it go?"

"I just gave him a scare, is all."

Cherif lets out a smoky sigh of relief.

"You afraid I'd kill him?"

He gives me an even look. "No idea. Maybe. You seemed to have it in for him."

"I just wanted it to be over with. I didn't know what I was doing—no, I did, I knew I couldn't kill him. I could never do a thing like that."

He claps me on the shoulder. "Forget all those assholes—"

"She's pregnant."

"What?"

"She's pregnant."

"How do you know?"

"Her husband called to tell me. He was over the moon."

"Are—"

"No, it wasn't me. It's been over three months, he said."

"And she knew?"

"No. She just found out. That's how they got to her. She was afraid for her kid...and for me. Eric said he'd kill her if she didn't do what he said."

"Goddamn—what a fucking mess! C'mon, let's have a drink."

At the bar, I remain silent for a few moments, staring at my beer and remembering: *I'm out. In front of the prison, no one's waiting. My father isn't here to pick me up. He said he'd never set foot near here. You can say a lot of things about the man, but one thing's for sure: he sticks to his word. I don't want to take the bus. I'll take a taxi, even if it costs me my right arm. The taxi driver's smoking a cigarette, leaning against the door of his car. He sees me coming. Without a word, he tosses his cigarette and gets inside. I get in the back. The radio's tuned to the news, an endless stream of opinion and conjecture about falling towers in New York.*

"Where to, boss?"

I give a start. I've forgotten how people talk outside.

"Paris."

I look out the dirty window at the street. I wait for the car to start up and the landscape to begin passing by, but nothing happens.

I straighten up and look at the driver, who turns his head my way.

"Where, exactly? Paris is a big place." He pauses, and his eyes get mean, then worried: "Hey, what's wrong with you?"

I realize I'm completely lost. And for maybe the first time in my life, I know exactly why I'm crying.

———————————

Outside the bar. Two a.m. Not a taxi in sight. I'm walking home. I'm drifting away when a voice rings out behind me.

"The fuck are you doing, Idir?" It's Cherif. He runs up.

"Going home."

"What, not even a good-bye?"

"I'm beat, I really need to go."

"C'mon, one more drink."

"No."

"One more drink and then I'll drive you home, OK? C'mon, dammit, don't make me beg." He puts an arm around my shoulders and leads me back to the bar.

"Just a quick one. Whisky."

"OK." He slaps my back. "Don't worry, Idir, everything'll be OK. Better this way."

So we go back in. After all, it doesn't cost me a thing to pretend he's not wrong.

Right about now, all I'm hoping is that I'll never feel moist dirt on my bare skin. And that when dawn comes, I'll walk over to my window after waking up alone in my bed and watch the sun hit the boulevard with everything it's got.

JÉRÉMIE GUEZ was born in Paris in 1988 and has already been hailed as the rising star of contemporary French noir. His two previous novels, *Balancé dans les cordes* and *Paris la unit*, were awarded the 2013 SNCF du Polar and 2012 Plume Libre prizes, respectively. *Eyes Full of Empty* is the highly anticipated first English translation of Jérémie Guez's work, and the third novel in his Parisian trilogy. He lives in Paris.

EDWARD GAUVIN is a prolific translator and the recipient of numerous awards. His work has been featured most recently in *The New York Times*, *Tin House*, *Best European Fiction 2014*, *PEN America*, *Words Without Borders*, and *Gigantic*, among others. He lives in San Jose, CA.